"We have to go," the man repeated. "But we can't just go. Do you know what I mean? We can't just go."

Dany's hope died stillborn.

"Give me the razor," he said, and she knew he wasn't talking to her anymore. It was stupid, of course, because the sock was around her eyes but she closed her eyes anyway so that she wouldn't see what he was doing because she was a stupid girl, as Roman always said, and that was the way she'd die.

At least she knew enough to pass out when he started . . .

GYPSY IN AMBER

Also by Martin Cruz Smith
Published by Ballantine Books:

GORKY PARK

GYPSY IN AMBER

MARTIN CRUZ SMITH

BALLANTINE BOOKS • NEW YORK

Library of Congress Catalog Card Number: 79-163416

ISBN 0-345-30614-7

Manufactured in the United States of America

First Ballantine Books Edition: October 1982

This book could not have been written without the help of the Gypsy library and the notes of Reverend Frederick S. Arnold.

For my father and mother

The Romany *chi*
And the Romany *chal*
Love *luripen*
And *lutchipen*
And *dukkeripen*
And *buknipen*
And every *pen*
But *moripen*
And *tatchipen*

The Gypsy woman
And the Gypsy man
Love stealing
And loving
And fortune-telling
And lying
And every *pen*
But killing
And truth

—OLD ROMANY SAYING

1

God made Man in His image, Roman had heard. He wondered which god would claim the body on the aluminum table.

"Caucasian female, age approximately twenty to twenty-five. Hair brown, eyes blue." The medical examiner spoke into a microphone clipped onto the lapel of his white smock. A wire from it led to the tape recorder in a roomy pocket.

"The body has been dismembered into six separate parts," he went on in a monotone. "Otherwise it appears to be that of a healthy female. All the teeth are present, although there are silver fillings on each of the upper right molars. There is a small, old diagonal scar under the chin. No digits are missing. There is some bruising of tissue on the knuckle of the fourth metacarpal, where a ring has been removed while alive or shortly afterward. There are no other scars, birthmarks or moles."

There were four men around the table. Roman wasn't a weak man; he'd seen death before. But the others, including Isadore, had professional objectivity to fall back on. He didn't, and the disassembled horror of the sterile room was a revelation to him. He'd never considered that put

1

back together, the human body resembled a misshapen octupus more than anything else.

The examiner had pulled back a flap of scalp and sawed through the skull for the brain. One cuff raised an eyelid to reveal a blue eye that stared at Roman with a madly askew iris.

"There is no sign of hematoma."

The brain, a convoluted ruby, was weighed and deposited in a glass jar. The examiner's assistant wrote out a label, licked the back and applied it to the jar.

Sergeant Harry Isadore looked out of place, a long-suffering snowman. His cheeks and nose were contrasting hues of blue and pink, and he slapped his thick hands together to encourage circulation. He had dressed for a warm summer day, and going into the mortuary on First Avenue had loosened his sinuses.

"You've got to admit it's easier this way," the assistant said as he pushed the legs and arms to one side.

The examiner opened the chest cavity and removed the heart and lungs and studied the interior of the cavity for fractured ribs. As a team, he and the assistant cut out the intestinal tract, the liver, spleen, pancreas and kidneys. When they had finished examining them, they placed the organs in glass-top fruit jars and sealed the tops with wax. The assistant wrote out more labels while the examiner drew blood for a typing, two men cataloguing a treasure.

The police reported the girl had come from the Cadillac Eldorado driven by Nanoosh Pulneshti. Nanoosh had started from Montevideo, Uruguay, gathering pieces for Roman. In Cuzco he bought Incan statuettes, in Manaus a crate of gold Empire service brought up the Amazon by a nineteenth-century rubber baron; in Maracaibo he stole silver candlesticks from an abandoned Jesuit fortress. He crossed the Rio Grande without passing through U.S. Customs, and three days later Nanoosh was on the Palisades Parkway approaching the George Washington Bridge. One of those everyday accidents occurred between the Eldorado and a U-Haul bringing antiques down from Newton, Massachusetts, to the Armory Show. Both Nanoosh and the U-Haul driver had died as the car jackknifed over the van. It would have been a simple case for the highway patrol except for the neat, scarcely bruised pieces of the girl they found strewn over the roadside.

"No spermatozoa," the assistant said after looking at a smear under the microscope.

"Can you give me a closer age, Doctor?" Isadore asked.

The examiner prodded the jaw open again while the assistant held the head steady.

"From the wear on the teeth"—he cut a thin line into the gum—"and the immaturity of the roots of the third molar, I would venture closer to twenty years than twenty-five." He pushed the jaw closed and shrugged. "She's not a virgin, but she's never borne a child or had an abortion. No evidence of drugs. Hardly any cavities. She must have been a clean liver."

Isadore had brought Roman down to identify Nanoosh in his stainless-steel filing cabinet. Roman didn't know what the point was in asking him to witness this gruesome theater. He refused to watch, looking instead at the curved tile floor with its black, grooved borders.

"*Rigor mortis* has set into the entire body. Since the face is still rigid, the victim may have been dead for from eighteen hours to twenty-four hours. However, there also seems to be little lividity, and the *in situ* report states that specimens of dry ice were found at the scene of the accident and it's possible the ice was used to preserve the body. So the time range can be stretched to about ten to thirty hours to account for the possible effect of a lower temperature on the muscles."

Roman cried for Nanosh, for the arrogance and daring reduced to a filing drawer. But this was another kind of reduction beyond grief, the butcher's secret.

"There are nine great wounds of dismemberment. Since there is a lack of bruises or lacerations to indicate a struggle, it is likely that separation of the head was first. The wound entry is from the back of the neck at the second cervical vertebra. The sinews and muscles are cleanly cut, and strands of the victim's hair are embedded in the flesh. Separation of the spinal cord, not to mention the jugular, indicates death was instantaneous. The weapon used was sharp, clean and heavy and used with great force. There is no indication of a second blow. The wound entries for dismemberment of the arms are at the armpits. The arms would appear to have been drawn back, and again there is no indication that more than one blow was used. In each case, the greater tubercles have been crushed. Likewise, the olecranons in the separation of the biceps from the forearms.

"The patella was shattered in each leg in the separation of the thighs from the calves. Separating the thigh from the pelvis was not such an easy matter. The thigh appears to have been spread back, and the wound entry is in front at the origin of the *rectus femoris;* but the neck of the *fovea capitus* seems to have resisted, particularly in the right leg, and several blows were necessary to disengage the femus from the pelvis.

"There are no in-and-out wounds to describe the assailant's weapon. There are no marks indicating a point on it. The assailant appears to have had a basic knowledge of anatomy and great strength. There are no hesitation wounds."

At the end of all this the examiner paused and glanced at Isadore. His assistant was at the ready, rolling forward a tray with its container of formalin, alcohol and carmine to embalm the parts. Isadore stopped the tray. He took a toothpick and ran its flat end under the girl's polished fingernails. He held the toothpick up to the light and inspected it.

"Nothing. She didn't suspect a thing. She thought she was with a friend."

"Is that all, Sergeant? We'd like to clean up."

"Hold it." He gestured for Roman. "One last thing."

Roman stood next to Isadore above the cool table with its display of meat.

"Is she Gypsy?" Isadore asked.

There was no way of avoiding it now. Roman looked, concentrating on minute points, refusing the whole. Finally, he looked at the fingernails Isadore had just held.

"No. There'd be a brown moon around the cuticle at the very least."

"Then how do you explain it?" Isadore asked.

"Explain what?"

"How she could think your friend Nanoosh was her friend?"

Roman didn't know what to say. Isadore was Roman's friend, too.

2

There were five faces visible in the window of "R. Grey—Antiques" when Isadore parked in front of it that morning. One was of a Siennese madonna, the perfect oval of her face outlined by her black hood, the hood set in a golden halo. The wings of joyous seraphim touched her shoulders as she ascended to heaven.

On the other side of the window was a Florentine banker captured in all his intelligent avarice. A rich fur hat mimicked the hands that weighed gold coins, and a greyhound's luminescent eyes watched the glittering money. In a corner was the inscription in red "bottega di Ghirlandaio."

Next to the sixteenth-century banker was another who could have been his brother, except that this head was set on shoulders of Dunhill pinstripe, and it was alive. Isadore recognized the senior member of the board of the American Stock Exchange as the man ran his hand tenderly down the carved frame. A look of anxiety was in the senior member's rimless glasses, and Isadore got an inkling of the painting's value. The fourth face was Roman's, and it was

a Byzantine and mysterious as the madonna's. The fifth
was that of Beng, Roman's solid black cat that paced from
one painting to the other.

The stock market was down. Isadore didn't know how
much until Roman put his arm around the broker's shoulders the way a sweetshop owner would put his arm around
a penniless boy. Beng disappeared from the window, a
sign that the bargaining was over. If it had been any other
Gypsy, Isadore would have been alert for a traveling wallet. With Roman he knew the customer would end up
signing a check eagerly another day, and in the meantime
Isadore couldn't help enjoying the tableau. The Gypsy was
one of his few indulgences.

When the broker had left with one last lingering pause
in front of the window, Isadore gave himself a second to
erase the smile from his lips. It wasn't a funny day. He got
out of his car slowly, for once not wanting to talk to the
dealer, taking in the narrow, expensive East Side street
with its picture townhouses where newsboys delivered the
Times and *Women's Wear Daily* in foyers.

The door to Roman's shop did not have an automatic
lock, making it a curiosity in the New York antique trade.

"*Sarishan*," Roman said. "I saw the long arm of the law
skulking across the street, so I put some tea on."

He was in the back of the shop barely visible past a
Chinese screen, but Isadore could see him grinning as he
set two cups and saucers beside a teapot.

"Morning," Isadore replied. He wasn't in the mood to
reciprocate their usual greeting. Roman came to the front
of the store with the cups. He had an exaggerated frown.

"Official business again. I never knew police work was
so dull until I met you, Sergeant."

"Hot tea, Christ," Isadore muttered. "On a day like today. It's already eighty out there." Just holding the saucer
made Isadore sweat.

"You're turning into a dilettante on me," Roman told
him taking a healthy sip from his cup. He pushed a chair
over to Isadore with his foot.

"Incidentally, what are those paintings worth?" Isadore
asked. He refused to sit, another compromise with his job.
He would have put the cup down on the table next to him,
but he didn't want to leave a ring.

"Whatever I can get. Michelangelo's teacher may have done the portrait if that gives you an idea."

"And you just leave them in the window?"

"I put them there so the customer could see them in daylight. I don't usually handle paintings, so I don't have any place to hang them."

"Yeah." Isadore looked around the interior. It had the haphazard jumble of a pawnshop; but he'd learned the prices of some of the pieces, and Roman had explained the salutary effect of the mess on the clientele's imagination. Inlaid chests lined the walls under suspended side chairs, partially unrolled tapestries and showcases of Oriental porcelain. It always reminded him of a museum tilted on its side.

"These paintings just sort of came into hand like everything else," he asked.

"Is that all it is?" Roman said. "You want to see the bills of sale? Why didn't you say so when you came in?"

"No." Isadore sighed and sat down. He rested his cup on his lap. "Look, what was Nanoosh Pulneshti doing for you?"

Roman tried to read the cop's face, but Isadore was staring at his tea.

"Nothing. Nanoosh is a friend of mine, you know that. What's the matter, is he in trouble?"

"Not anymore. He's dead."

Isadore looked up, trying to catch Roman's reaction. It was too late; all he saw was brown mask calm. If it had been another Rom bringing the news, Roman would have cried openly. For a callous moment Isadore found himself resenting the limits on friendship between Rom and *gajo*, but he went on.

"He died in a car accident. Witnesses say he was trying to get onto the exit ramp for the George Washington Bridge the same time as a van. You know what happens: Neither one wanted to give way, so they're both dead now."

"Nanoosh was a good driver."

"Maybe the other driver was at fault. So what? The thing is, we found another body in Nanoosh's car. A girl, she'd been murdered. Brunette, pretty, I don't think she's Gypsy. Young, blue eyes."

"What are you driving at?" Roman asked. Isadore kept his face averted to keep from clueing him.

"You might know who she is. I want you to take a look at her; it's as simple as that."

Roman shrugged. Beng threaded his way through a set of Meissen.

"I don't know what you're talking about, Sergeant. Besides, how do you know the girl wasn't killed in the accident?"

"Take a look at her and you'll know. The bastard was carting her around the whole day, Roman. Maybe he was a pal of yours; but Nanoosh didn't have a driver's license, the plates on the car were bad, and he had a knife."

"What's wrong with that?"

"They're wrong to me. I'm not trying to pin this on him just because of that, though. We found a whole bunch of stuff from his car all over the road. Silver plates, candlesticks, statues. And the girl. His Cadillac was split open like a beer can."

"Then you didn't find her in Nanoosh's car."

Beng had settled beside a ceramic view of the Rhine and glared at Isadore.

"Not in it, no. You don't put a seat belt on a corpse."

"And the other car?"

"It was a small truck, a U-Haul. That was open, too, but no luck. It was checked from top to bottom right before the crash by an insurance examiner. That's the problem, Roman; no insurance examiners are around when your friends are delivering antiques to you. You operate differently."

"There were antiques in the van?"

"Yes."

"That's interesting. You don't think so?"

"No. Damn it, Roman, this isn't a game. I came here to tell you that the delivery boy in your little operation has killed somebody. I know how you got that chandelier over there and that tapestry. I haven't been able to prove it; but I know, and maybe I wasn't trying hard enough because it was only a matter of you milking a few snobs. This time it's murder. Nanoosh was bringing his cargo to you, body and all."

"There are over a thousand antique dealers between Wall Street and Eighty-sixth Street."

"But you're the only Gypsy. He was coming here, this shop."

"The only Gypsy," Roman repeated. He looked at Isadore with some sorrow. "That's why you came here. Are you going to arrest me because I'm the only Gypsy?"

"That's not what I meant, and you know it. Do you deny that you operate outside the law for the stuff you sell? Come on, be honest with me."

"As a friend? No, I won't deny I operate outside your laws. As a suspect I deny everything. Now I get a question. This accident didn't happen in New York. It happened in New Jersey—didn't it?—while Nanoosh was getting on the bridge for the city. What have the New York police and you got to do with it?"

It took a moment for Isadore to answer, but there was no chance for evasion. Roman already knew the answer.

"They gave it to us because I'm the Gypsy expert," Isadore said. "They thought you'd talk to me."

Roman left without a word and went to the rear of the store. Isadore sat in his chair feeling angry and foolish. The shock of Nanoosh's death hadn't worked, and the threat about the merchandise had failed as miserably as the first time he tried it when Roman opened the store years ago. Beng leaped from the porcelain to the top of a secretary desk. The cat looked at Isadore complacently, then shut its eyes and went to sleep. Its whiskers looked almost white against its fur. Isadore, the Gypsy expert, remembered that Beng was named for the devil of the Ganges. Otherwise, he knew as much about the cat as he did about its owner. Roman came back and dropped an ice cube into Isadore's cup.

"You should have told me before you wanted your tea another way," he said. He wiped his dark hands on a handkerchief.

"If you want some help, here it is," he went on. "Nanoosh was a Gypsy, just like me. He broke laws. He stole cars, and he liked girls, too. Gypsy girls. But he was no killer. You have my word."

A Gypsy's word, Isadore thought. That was like a contradiction. On the other hand, Roman Grey was a contradiction.

"That's not enough."

"That's all you're going to get. Nanoosh didn't waste his time with *gaja*; he trusted only Gypsies. As for *gaja* women he despised them; he said they were milk, and a *gaja* man was a thief who made his own rules. He wouldn't touch either of them. If you want to find out who killed the girl, you look for her kind of man."

"So far as I know, you're an accomplice to murder," Isadore said. He was out of his chair, and his face was flushed. He looked for some place to put the cup down.

"I don't have anything left to say to you, Sergeant. That's a Hancock Worcester you have in your hand; try not to break it." He took the cup from Isadore.

"I could pull you in right now. You've already admitted dealing in unregistered antiques."

"That's too bad," the Gypsy said. "You were one *gajo* I trusted."

Isadore's hand had reflexively gone to his chrome cuffs for the arrest when the shop door opened. A girl came in. She was dressed in Saks' version of a fringed Indian dress, and she wore a beaded headband around her brown hair. She was beautiful and vaguely familiar. It wasn't just that Isadore had the sense he'd seen her on a dozen television commercials. She was what all his son's dates tried to look like.

"Roman, did you know how many calories there are in goulash?" she demanded.

Roman winced and relaxed slightly. He leaned on the secretary.

"Thousands," she said, "literally thousands. If I had any, it would be dry toast for a month. That's what they feed prisoners."

"Dany, it was your idea," Roman said. "You wanted to cook a real Hungarian dish."

"But goulash?" the girl asked Isadore. "Have you ever seen those Hungarian girls? No wonder they all look like sausages. You never see French girls eating goulash."

"I don't think my friend is interested in your peculiar view of nationalities," Roman told her.

"A friend?" The girl's attitude changed from distress to

pleasure. She seized Isadore's hand. "I'm so glad to meet you. Roman never introduces me to any of his friends. He thinks they'll disapprove," she said in a stage whisper. "I never would have thought you were a Gypsy."

"He's not," Roman said. "Dany Murray, meet Sergeant Harry Isadore. He's a policeman."

Her attitude went back to distress. She retracted her hand.

"I haven't said anything wrong, have I?" she asked Roman.

"Nothing they can send me up for, unless there's a law against consorting with gibbering clotheshorses."

"Maybe I'll be going," she suggested.

Roman nodded. She kissed him quickly on the cheek and just as quickly wiped it off with her hand.

"He hates lipstick," she told Isadore. On her way out the door she stopped long enough to say, "Poached eggs," and was gone before Roman could answer.

He rubbed his face and turned back to the policeman. He could see that Isadore had thought of something new.

"Well, Sergeant, aren't you going to arrest me?"

"No, It's just that there's another *gaja* girl I want you to meet."

3

Sergeant Isadore inhaled and coughed. He was trying to give up cigarettes by smoking small cigars, but he kept forgetting. As he pounded himself on the chest, he wondered whether his son was going to keep his student deferment. Perhaps if he keeled over in Captain Frank's office, they'd let Morris stay home as a hardship case. That was a hell of a price to pay to keep a son home.

"You ought to give up smoking," Frank suggested balefully.

"I know," Isadore said. He stubbed out the cigar in the stand-up ashtray the city provided.

"Now tell me again. Is it Roman Grey or Romano Gry? Which one is the alias?"

"Both," Isadore said. "I mean they're both his real names. Gry is his name with other Gypsies. Grey is for *gaja*, non-Gypsies."

"This is a simple case, Sergeant. But I'm beginning to see what makes it complicated." Frank had the almost hairless head of a newborn bird, and it lolled from side to side as he spoke. "If I remember correctly, we've spoken about him before."

"He's cooperated with the department before, Captain."

"Sergeant, I'd call donating some chairs for the Police-men's Ball swell, but I wouldn't call it cooperation."

"Yes," Isadore agreed. "Well, we don't have enough in-formation to make a charge stick. He can account for his whereabouts for the past four days, we can't get any com-plaints from his customers, and actually we haven't established any provable link between Pulneshti and Grey."

Frank squinted at the one-by-two-inch photo of Grey stapled to his file. "Looks like some kind of mulatto to me."

"The Grys are famous for being dark," Isadore pointed out. "They're Lovari Gypsies like Pulneshti. Grey has quite an interesting background. Orphaned and brought up by a judge in New York. That's where he got the money to start his store."

"How about that? Can you tell me anything about the girl or Pulneshti? Something dull like the murder?"

Isadore swallowed a cough. "Nothing positive. The FBI can't match her prints, and it takes some time to check all the runaways and missing persons. The lab tests verified no hard drugs, so we're hitting the missing persons harder. Pulneshti has a record of grand and petty larceny, mostly cars, but we don't have any record of next of kin."

Frank snapped his middle finger on the Grey file. "No help here?"

"No. He says he's sure we'll catch the guilty party."

For a man whose avocation was sarcasm, Frank was not alert to the possibility in others. He merely grunted.

"We're trying to cut down the area of search," Isadore continued. "We sent a description of the car around the national wire, and we have a zoologist looking at it tomor-row to check out the bugs on the car and the radiator. That could help us determine where the car's been, and it certainly looks as if it's been everywhere."

Frank's face was starting to screw up with an inner pain.

"It's a little unorthodox, I know," Isadore said, "but it's not like tracing an ordinary person. Gypsies don't carry credit cards, they don't stay at motels, they don't have bank accounts, and they don't talk to the police. Even when they do talk, it's in their own language. None of the usual techniques work."

Frank looked at Isadore for a long time. They'd started out in the Police Academy together, and Isadore had always gotten the better marks; he was the one who was expected to rise to inspector. Instead, Frank had followed orders, never hounded a case too long, always remembered St. Patrick's Day, and now he was ahead by two grades and a few thousand dollars. Still, they had an understanding.

"Harry, we've got to wrap this case up fast. It's practically done for us. Pulneshti was probably the killer, and he's dead. But the commissioner is resigning. The Irishman at the Central Investigation Department wants the job. So does the Jew at the Detective Bureau. The district attorneys and the captains are lining up with their boys, and I've got to jump soon. I thought I could lay low until this girl and the Gypsy came along in Jersey. Now someone transferred this homicide to you and me and I don't know who. It sounds like that college boy at the bureau, but CID is closer to the Jersey patrol. If you handle this right one of them is going to take the credit. Unless they expect you to blow it and then they can pin it on the other."

"Why don't you call one of them and find out?"

"The phone's tapped, that's why. I tried to get messages through, but they're both traveling all over town with their flying squads. Do you understand? You have to wrap this up fast and neat, and if it means putting this other Gypsy in the can for a while, I'll back you up. Until we find out who comes out on top."

Frank pushed the files across the desk to Isadore.

"You're the man with the imagination, think up something," Frank said. "Anyway, from what you tell me, we're dealing with born criminals."

4

On West Eighty-second Street above a *bodega* with a Puerto Rican flag flying over cans of papaya juice and bottles of saffron was an even more colorful window. It had a yellow hand with red lifelines dealing the ace of spades. Hanging out over the street was a sign with smaller versions of the symbols and the words "Madame Vera. Fortunes told in your hands, in the cards. Love or Career. What is Fate?"

Madame Vera had moved to the *ofisa* a month before. She and her family of twelve had driven over the Manhattan Bridge from their old *ofisa* on Flatbush Avenue in Brooklyn in two new but battered Chryslers. When they arrived at their new business address, the girls immediately unloaded a stack of folding chairs from the trunks. The men brought up tables, and the boys struggled up stairs with *gonyas*. Each *gonya* consisted of a strap that went over the shoulders with enormous bags at each end. Inside was all the wealth of the family in heavy necklaces of American eagles, double eagles, old Mexican pesos even richer in gold, but mostly Austrian four ducats with the head of Emperor Franz Josef. As the tables and chairs

19

were set up, the men strode up and down the stairs with bedrolls and the eiderdown quilts called *dunbas*.

While the men relaxed with cigarettes, Vera and her sisters and daughters prepared the *ofisa*. They hammered nails into the walls, strung wires from the nails, and hung dark-red curtains from the wires so that in a matter of minutes the railroad flat was divided into living quarters and tearooms where the women could do their *duikkerin*, fortune-telling. Three crudely painted oilcloths were hung. One displayed a hand with the tracery of a map, another a buddha and a cross, and the third a phrenologist's chart. Along the walls were tacked horoscope magazines and newspaper clippings on Django Reinhardt and Yul Brynner. Altogether, it took an hour to prepare the *ofisa* for its customers.

Customers demanded such a setting. They climbed the stairs anxious about dreams or curious about a number to play. Only a few asked about their future. Holding their hand, Vera would usually satisfy them with, if they were old, "a dispute over property that has caused great anguish" or, if they were young, "your passions have been misunderstood and got you in great trouble." The different ones with real secrets could be read, too, though. The way they spoke, whether their eyes could stay with hers, the corner of a mouth were all letters in an alphabet that merely needed to be put into words and then sentences.

The family would stay in the *ofisa* until Vera made her *bozur*. Vera would know the victim as soon as she entered, a woman alone whose children visited once a month, just like the last one in Brooklyn. Vera had spent more time than usual in sympathetic conversation before abruptly asking whether this woman suffered from peculiar pains lately. Like all the victims, she agreed eagerly. Vera examined her palm carefully and saw "something bad." She sent the woman home and told her to sleep naked under her three warmest blankets holding an egg over her belly. The next day the woman returned with the egg wrapped in a napkin. Vera broke the egg open and lying in the yolk was a tiny hideous head with human hair grinning up at them. The devil's head was proof of the evil—possibly cancer—growing inside her. It was the sign of a curse.

The root of the curse was the money in the woman's

savings account. Vera explained that at some time it had passed through the hands of a murderer and the evil would only stop growing when she had taken the curse off. She wanted no payment for herself; this was too important a matter. As a test, she told the woman to draw a ten-dollar bill from her account and bring it to her with another egg in a napkin.

When the woman came back, she tried to give the bill to Vera, but the Gypsy refused to touch it. She asked the woman to place the napkin in a corner of the *ofisa*. They waited an hour, and when they broke the egg, looking up at them was another ugly devil's head. There was no longer any doubt about the curse.

Vera told the woman what was necessary. The next day she went to her bank and drew out evey cent in her savings account in large denominations, fifties and hundreds, "so that it will fit in the little bag," as Vera put it. The Romani word for the little bag of money was *bozur*, and Vera would have to hold it when she took the curse off.

The woman tied up the *bozur* herself. While she gaped, Vera began talking to the bag and to the special spirits she was in contact with. Soon the talking turned to pleading, the English turned to Romani and then to complete unintelligibility as the Gypsy collapsed on the floor, rolling her eyes and moaning under the force of the *bozur*. She ripped her blouse and scratched her face. As she yielded a particularly eerie howl of agony, her hands slipped the bag into her several thicknesses of petticoats and a second, absolutely similar bag appeared. At last, Vera passed out on the floor.

When she was revived, she had bad news for the woman. The curse could be drawn off, but only if the money were destroyed. When the woman hesitated, the Gypsy pointed to the devil's head that leered at them from a glass case. Vera had the bucket and coals ready when the woman gave in. The victim threw the *bozur* in herself, a phony *bozur* with paper cut in the shape of bills, and the two women knelt and prayed as the flames shot up. Finally, Vera told the woman that she was saved but only on the condition that she never tell anyone how.

Of course, the following day the bank manager called the woman's sons, and they got the full story from her;

but by then Madame Vera and her family had moved their *gonyas* and *dunbas* into a new *ofisa*.

Today, however, a prospective victim would have been disappointed. For once, fate had cheated Madame Vera.

"*Nanoosh, te aves yertime mander, te yertil tut o Del,*" Roman said. He was in the center of the long *ofisa*. Dark curls hung over his face, and his suit was torn and damp with sweat.

"Nanoosh, if you will forgive me all I have done to you, I will forgive all you have done to me." The chorus came from the figures huddled along the walls of red burlap.

"*Te avel angla tute, Nanoosh, kodo khabe tai kado pimo tai mange pe sastimaste,*" Vera Pulneshti said. Tears ran over the deep lacerations on her cheeks.

"Nanoosh, if you will forgive me all I have done to you, I will forgive all you have done to me," the family repeated. In a small pile in the center of the room was whatever jewelry they had been wearing when they heard of Nanoosh's death. Roman's cuff links were mixed with earrings and necklaces. In the gloom, they reflected the votive candles lit on a small altar that carried a photo of Nanoosh and a miniature figure of a Black Virgin.

One of the children, a girl with a mat complexion, passed around a tray of tea sweetened with strawberry jam. It would be all the Pulneshtis were allowed to eat until after the burial. Roman took a glass, holding it with his thumb on the rim and his forefinger on the bottom. Vera refused a glass for herself and held onto Roman's arm.

"He was such a good man. You remember how you respected him. Everyone respected him," she said hoarsely.

It wasn't exactly true. Nanoosh was a gambler, good at the races but bad at cards, and he owed everybody. But he was great fun at a party, and he played the guitar like a Gitano, and it was his sister's duty to see him praised.

"Those things I said to Nanoosh the last time you were here? That was love talking, you understand. And now he's dead."

When Roman tried to comfort her, she pushed him away. She waddled ferociously to the makeshift altar and snatched the picture to bring back to Roman. It was a Polaroid snapshot of Nanoosh sitting on the fender of a limousine.

"He was a great Rom," Roman said soothingly. The other men in the room grunted agreement.

"Is this the face of a murderer?" Vera asked. "Can this man have killed some stupid *gaji* and cut her into pieces? No! Are you going to tell me that, Romano Gry?"

"I didn't," Roman said. "The police are fools, but they'll find out that Nanoosh had nothing to do with it." He believed what he said. Isadore was like all *gaja*, collectors hoarding pieces of a style or a crime. Sooner or later, it would become obvious that Nanoosh was a piece that didn't fit. Whether Isadore found out who did commit the crime, he didn't care.

"Then why did they come to you?" Vera asked, advancing on him. With her eyes burning between the tangle of her hair and the red stripes on her cheeks, she was undeniably formidable.

"You know how they are. They wanted to know where Nanoosh was going and they thought I could help them."

Vera's heavily sagging front had Roman's back against a window. He had heard that not even the most skeptical client left her *ofisa* without a twenty-dollar scare.

"Ah! Then they thought you could help," she said.

"He was bringing some things to me, you know." He looked around to see if one of the men would pull Vera off him. There wasn't a chance; she had the whole family cowed. Her son Tibo in the corner could lift a small car to remove its transmission. Around his mother he was a mouse. Even the Welfare Department paid Vera just to keep her out of the office.

"Look, I've fixed it so that you can pick up Nanoosh and give him a decent burial," Roman told her.

"A decent burial!" she shrieked. Vera turned to the rest of the room so that everyone could appreciate her histrionics equally. "Listen to Romano. A decent burial! My brother is called a murderer, and this man says we will have a decent burial!" She spit on the floor. "You live like the *gaja* so much that you're turning into one. What about Nanoosh's *mulo*? What about tonight when his spirit walks around that cold morgue knowing that the shame of a murder is on him?"

There was nothing ridiculous in what she was saying. Nanoosh's spirit was freed from his body, dead but not gone, a *mulo*. The *gaja* might despise the Romany, but no Rom ever forgot his dead. For him, roaming over the earth were not only the half million Gypsies who drew breath but also the countless Gypsies who had gone before, restless spirits still wandering through cities and deserts, still real. In the dark room hung with Vera's maroon curtains this was a fact.

All the same, Roman suppressed a smile. Vera was flaunting her dramatic talents. She shuddered, displaying her strong profile. Her large hook nose was almost as fine as Roman's.

"Nanoosh made only one mistake," she announced. "He thought that Romano was a true Rom, a *phral*. Perhaps it's better he never knew that he was wrong. As you all know, a Gypsy girl is not good enough for this man here. He doesn't dress like a Gypsy or eat like one or smell like one to me. We are not worth his bother. He's changed. I'm sorry, Nanoosh, forgive me for telling you."

Roman sighed. "Okay, Vera, what are you after? Just tell me."

The fortune-teller let her bosom stop heaving and wiped a tear from her eye. "I only want you to help the *mulo* of your friend. Nanoosh can never reach paradise with the taint of murder on his name. The police asked you to help. I think they're right, the ignorant bastards. You do that. You prove that Nanoosh was an honest man, that he didn't kill anybody."

Roman didn't see how he could ever prove Nanoosh was honest, but he said, "I'll see what I can do."

"That's better," Vera said. On cue, one of her daughters came out of the shadows with a paper plate. On it was a pastry dripping with pistachio and honey. "We can't eat until the *pomana*," she said, "but you should. You have a lot of work ot do."

"Thanks." He noticed that Vera was her old self now that she had gotten her way.

"Why are you grinning like a fool?" she asked.

"For the best of reasons," Roman answered.

5

Nanoosh's burial was at a cemetery in Linden, New Jersey, where New York Gypsies had for years buried their dead. Isadore watched at a distance, but Vera was unable to restrain herself from sinking to her knees in the freshly turned soil and reaching down to her brother's coffin. The mourners spoke in Romani, and Isadore was able to catch only a few phrases. As the gravediggers began throwing the dirt on the coffin, the Gypsies threw money so that a rich mix of earth and money lay over Nanoosh. The Gypsies got back into their Cadillacs and headed north to New York. Roman walked over to Isadore, who was waiting in his Ford.

"You want a ride back?" Isadore asked.

"I was hoping for it," Roman said. He got into the car. "Did you hear anything?"

"You know I can't speak it that well."

They rode up U.S. 1 past Roselle and Hillside on New Jersey's sprawling checkerboard of suburbs and industrial slums. Isadore's hat was pushed back to reveal a white untanned line. He drove conscientiously with both hands on the wheel as he discussed his son, whom he was taking to watch the Mets at Shea Stadium on the weekend.

"I want to prove that there's more to life than protest meetings," Isadore said.

"The Mets are really up there, aren't they?" Roman asked absentmindedly. "They're ahead of the Jets, right?"

Isadore's mouth dropped in shock. "Jets? That's a football team. Boy, you really aren't in contact with the real world, are you?" He glanced at his passenger with a very fast, very safe jerk of his head to see if he was being kidded. "You do know that baseball is the national pastime, don't you?"

'Baseball, football, Jets, Mets . . ." Roman looked out the window at a large sign going by. It claimed that New Jersey had more paved highway per acre than any other state in the nation. "Anything more on the girl?"

"No fingerprints on file, so we have to wait on the dental records. That means we have to find out where she came from. We'll find out, just like we'll find out where the car was coming from. Nanoosh had it full of goods from South America. The captain said it didn't mean anything because there was no report from customs on Nanoosh. I think I've finally convinced him that Gypsies have been crossing borders for a long time without going through customs. As soon as we get an answer from our zoologist on the bugs found on the car, we'll know exactly where it's been. Amazing what those experts can do, find an ant caught in amber that's been dead, extinct for a million years, and they can tell you all about it. We'll trace the car, and we'll find the girl."

"So you still think it was Nonoosh."

"Damn it, Roman, who else could it be?"

They drove on for another mile bordered by streams colored by chemicals.

"Which means that I'm the best suspect you have," Roman pointed out.

"Something like that."

Isadore chewed on his lower lip for want of a cigarette. He was suffering, Roman saw. He had a murder, and he was a good cop, and he should be making an arrest, at least for the record.

"Look at it from my viewpoint, Roman. Antiques and

objects of art have to be declared when they enter the country. The United States has agreements with these countries your friends go through, and if you don't take their stuff out through legal channels, it's contraband. You're the head of a contraband ring. Nanoosh is your accomplice, and he kills a girl. Maybe it was an accident, but he chopped her up afterward." Isadore glanced at Roman again. "Nanoosh was your accomplish, and he butchered her."

The Ford looped around a tractor and continued on.

"I can just forget about it, say it's closed. New York has one unsolved murder a day. Just statistics, one more statistic. But the girl was mutilated. How can I face my son if I do that? Answer me."

"What would you like me to do?"

"Help me." Isadore was almost pleading. "I don't think you knew anything about the girl, but just tell me what you know. I can get you off the contraband rap pretty light. Those bills of sale you have aren't too bad."

The chubby hands gripping the wheel were turning white. Ahead of them Newark was rising mirage-like on heat waves. The glass slab of an insurance company towered over a ghetto. The dull cube of a brewery floated in a yeasty fragrance in the center of the city. The Ford followed the stream of cars toward the tunnels for Manhattan.

"Tell you what," Roman said. "Get on the turnpike for the Palisades and we'll try to see what happened."

Isadore thought it over. Taking the Gypsy in would please Frank, and it might even ease his own conscience. He was still telling himself he was considering it when he got on the turnpike at Kearny. The turnpike led through the steel bubbles of oil refineries to Fort Lee and the Palisades Parkway. A stench of oil that was like the stench of a decaying animal made them shut the windows of the car. Roman lit a Gauloise to kill the taste. Isadore refused one.

The Palisades Parkway was tidy and landscaped in comparison to the turnpike. The George Washington Bridge made a neat paperweight at its southern end. White on green notices urged drivers to park and enjoy the view of the Hudson. Isadore made a U-turn through a gap in the

median strip marked "For Official Use Only" and pulled
up on the side of the road.

"What do you expect to find?" Isadore asked.

"I don't know."

They got out and walked along the gravel skirt, moving
in slow motion against the lane of cars at their side. Isadore pointed to white scrapes in the concrete. In a direct
line across the river was the medieval arcade of the Clois-
ters.

"That's where the van turned over. You'd see some
blood around here, but the state cleans up after highway
accidents now. I can show you photos if you want to see
what the stains and the cars looked like."

Roman kicked the gravel around with the toe of his
shoe. At once, he realized how silly it was to think he
would find something in the stones that the police had
missed. Riders took mildly curious stares at him as the
cars continued to roll by a few feet away toward the
bridge. He wandered off onto the grass bank. If there were
something the cops had missed, it would be gone by now.
The grass was freshly mown. He rubbed his hand over his
chin. Stubble was already growing back from the morning
shave. Some people couldn't keep as freshly mown.

Isadore walked back to the car. He didn't mind
watching someone discover how hard it was to play a real
detective, but he didn't want to embarrass a friend. He
came back with a manila envelope closed with twine.

"These are the pictures, Roman. They'll help you." He
opened the envelope and took out twenty eight-by-ten
glossies.

"Thanks."

The first shots had been taken from the top of the police tow truck, and they showed a hundred yards of road.
The van was nearest, on its side. The Cadillac was
sprawled about twenty yards beyond it, upside down. Instead of bodies, X's marked where they had been picked
up. Far down the road and on either side were pieces of
furniture and plates, and ropes and padding. Roman
remembered that it had been a sunny day. The gold plates
shined. Among them were other X's marking where different parts of the girl's body had been found.

Most of the other photos were close-ups of the cars and

of the bodies with blankets drawn back as they rested in useless ambulances. Worst were the pictures of the anonymous girl, each part of her in its plastic bag on a separate picture complete with six-inch celluloid markers so that the mind couldn't help guessing—as if it were a game—which part was which. Roman looked from the photos to the road. A sports car without a muffler was racing over the spot where her head was picked up.

"See." Isadore's finger pointed to the first photo of the road. "Plates, bits of statue, the girl. All in the same area."

"And the antiques."

"And one big difference between the way you operate and the way Hoddinot Sloan operates. His antiques were going to his stall at the Armory Show. An agent from his insurance company got in the van in Nyack to check the whole shipment inside and out. That's why the van was using the Palisades instead of staying on the Merritt. The agent even followed the van on the parkway for a few miles, and we have witnesses in other cars who happened to see him all the way to the accident. It's too bad nobody checks you out."

Isadore waited in the car while Roman policed the side of the road with the photos. Finally, the Gypsy gave up and joined him.

"Well, what's your answer?" Isadore asked. "Are you going to help?"

"This Sloan," Roman said. He seemed surprisingly undiscouraged as he knocked another cigarette out of his pack. "Has he picked up his antiques?"

Isadore rolled his fingertips on the wheel once and turned the car into the traffic. "No. Why should he sweat it? He probably made a profit off the insurance, and his antiques are a mess. Besides, there's some question of who can release them. We have it in town, but New Jersey is still carrying it on paper. Typical foul-up."

"He hasn't looked at his antiques himself?"

"We sent him some photos through the Massachusetts police. He identified them and said they were total losses, which you don't have to be an expert to see. I spoke to him on the phone, and frankly, he's a bastard. Didn't even ask how the driver was."

"What about the driver?"

Isadore sighed. He tapped a paper bag that hung under the police radio. Up to now Roman had thought it was a litter bag. It was Isadore's file. Inside were business envelopes stuffed with notes.

"That's the one," Isadore said.

"Locher" was written in longhand on the envelope Roman held. He opened it and took out sheets of paper held together by a paper clip. In six pages Isadore had a concise record of Harold "Buddy" Locher from birth to death at twenty-nine. There were medical, psychological and vocational descriptions, most of them concerning his life in the Army. He'd mustered out as a corporal ten days before at Fort Hood, Texas.

On the back of the last page Isadore's longhand made its second appearance. "Locher left the service to avoid a third tour of Vietnam. He claims (see Psych.) to be a mechanic, not an infantryman. Arrival in Boston one day before accident looking for friend who was out of town. Got job driving where friend worked on friend's route because short of drivers. In Boston one night sleeping at friend's place. Witnesses verify he was alone. Picks up loaded van in Boston, van checked in Nyack, N.Y., seen all the way to bridge exit and acc. No motive or opportunity."

Roman looked through the middle pages before stuffing the notes back into the envelope. "Very thorough. No motive, no opportunity."

"Right. You're beginning to learn I don't just sit on my ass and harass Gypsies. Locher was a little nutty, if that's what you can call being afraid of dying. Even if he was a homicidal maniac, though, he didn't have a chance to prove it."

They coasted off the George Washington Bridge and curled onto the Henry Hudson Parkway. There was an envelope on himself, Roman knew. Skimpy on the background but heavy on suspicion. Suspect for being a Gypsy but not acting like one, which was a different kind of double jeopardy. Would Isadore be amused that for a long time he had worked at piecing his own past together?

Everyone knew about the Jews killed by the Nazis. No one knew or cared about the five hundred thousand Gypsies slaughtered in camps because "for reasons of public health and particularly because the Gypsies have manifestly a heavily tainted heredity, and because they are inveterate criminals who constitute parasites in the bosom of our people, it is fitting to prevent them from reproducing themselves and to subject them to the obligation of forced labor in the labor camps. We must pursue this program fearlessly and unreservedly, keeping in mind that sterilization is but a half-measure. It is in conformity with the principles of a state with morals on a high level and particularly the Third Reich."

The letter from the *Gauleiter* of Steiermark to the *Reichsminister* was one Roman remembered well. It created the high-sounding paper trap that caught his parents and killed them either in a camp or some cattle car rolling from Rumania with other *Rassenverfolgte*, racial undesirables. His father and mother had been foolish, of course. They were English Gypsies, and they thought they could ignore the war and take to the road for the wedding of a friend outside Constanta. It was the time of the Phony War and Gypsies always ignored *gaja* affairs. They were in the middle of the celebration toasts when the *Sicherheitsdienst* threw a ring of truck lights on them and divided them into men and women and children and loaded them up for the short drive to the railroad junction.

There was no very good reason for his escape. The truck he was in was at the end of the line, and the security police didn't see any need yet for the rear guard of motorcycles they would use later when those rounded up knew where they were going. Because the truck was so crowded, the five-year-old boy sat with the driver and guard in front. Halfway to the station, the truck slowed down and the guard pushed him out onto a grassy bank. Then it sped up to rejoin the dark caravan, and that was the last time he ever saw his parents. Yojo and Mara Gry didn't exist anymore.

He walked back down the road to the deserted campsite because he didn't know where else to go. Roman sat in the middle of a scene that looked like an abandoned circus, the painted vans and tents and hungry, tethered horses and even a trained bear sprawling over the meadow in bewilderment, waiting for Gypsies. The only ones to come were an old couple of Turco-Americans who were late. They

understood immediately what had happened, and they
stayed only long enough to stuff Roman in the back of
their ancient car. Lazlo and Yula Kronitos had returned
from the United States with the money they'd made on
bozur so that they could roam through Anatolia comfortably. Instead, they headed through North Africa and then
to Portugal, paying their way with the infinite gold coins
of Yula's heavy necklaces, taking the boy with them.
From Lisbon they sailed to New York, where they gave
Roman to their son, and when the ship left to return to
Europe, the old couple was on it. The boy had been a
"heavenly obligation" in Yula's eyes, and they had dis-
charged it.

It was not difficult to gain American papers for Roman.
He retained his father's *gaja* name, Grey, because it fitted
well. He spoke English. Besides, the authorities had long
given up the battle of keeping birth certificates for Gypsy
children born on the road. When the police did question
his false papers of baptism, the Gypsies turned to another
defense. Roman became the court ward of a downstate
New York professor. It was a traditional ploy for a Gypsy
family to seek the protection of a sympathetic and wealthy
gajo. To be one of these was to be a *rai*. "Part sucker and
part father" was the way James Oliver described the title
he had gained. Oliver was a Poughkeepsie judge who'd left
the bench to study Sanskrit. His interest in Gypsies began
when he discovered the closeness between Romani and the
lost language, and he was a regular godfather at Gypsy
baptisms. It was not difficult to infiltrate a Gypsy boy into
his large empty house along the Hudson.

"What are you?" Oliver would muse aloud to the olive-
colored boy who sat across from him at the dinner table.
"East Indian? English? Not Turkish, I would guess despite
your friends. Rom, naturally, but Lovari or another tribe?
The English Grys are famous for being dark and clever, so
I suppose that fits. Then Rom, let's settle for that. But
when you leave, do you think you might be part *gajo*,
too?" And Roman would shake his head vigorously.

Oliver took a poorly hidden delight in tutoring the
bright boy in the things he considered important. His ten-
ure in the court had given him a distaste for politics and
the law. What he appreciated decorated his house, thou-

sands of books in a dozen languages and a priceless collection of antiques. "It's not so horrible that you've broken something," he told Roman as they stood amid the bright remains of a crystal goblet, "as the fact that you don't know what it is you've broken." Roman learned, mainly because what he broke he had to put back together under the careful direction of the professor.

Roman was nine when he ran away for the first time. He'd spent weeks out before with Gypsies coming through the Hudson Valley, but this time he was away for a year, wandering with a family of Kalderash as far as Mexico City. When he returned, he found a place set for him at the table. "Take the apologetic look off your face," Oliver said. "I wouldn't expect a *vadni ratsa* to stay in a pen." Roman picked up a piece of bread and smiled with relief. A *gajo* who understood "the wild goose" was a *rai* indeed.

The table was always set for him no matter how far or long he traveled, and when he was searching for the grave of his parents, out of concern for their *mule*, there were long absences. It was after walking over a field in Bavaria where the grass was growing again over the lime pits that he found a letter waiting at Munich General Delivery. Professor James Hancock Oliver had died of tuberculosis. Efforts to reach Roman by mail or through American consulates had been in vain. Would he return on receipt of this letter? He was the main beneficiary of Mr. Oliver's will. It was only rereading the letter a hundredth time—he was sitting beside the warm, dull Danube and cursing the *gaja* mails; if it had been a Rom who died, he would have known about it in a day no matter where he was—that he realized he'd wasted another father while he was looking for his first. He was twenty years old, and he was rich in exactly those things he didn't want. Otherwise, he had nothing.

"I'm going down to department headquarters, Roman," Isadore said. "Are you coming in with me or not?"

"Sure, Sergeant. I'd like to take a look at the Sloan antiques."

"Why? Sloan didn't."

Roman laughed. "I guess that's why."

6

The department warehouse was so crowded with crates of liquor, televisions, transistor radios and all the other criminal evidence of an affluent society that the guards in charge had long ceased trying to maintain order. The Sloan antiques made a small pile that was roped off from a tower of dusty clothes on one side and an unsteady stack of typewriter cases on the other.

"There you are," Isadore said. He was unconsciously dusting his pants as he walked. "Officer Swoboda will have to keep an eye on you, you understand. I don't know what you think you're going to find. Afterward, you'll come up and see me?"

"Thanks, Sergeant. I'll just look around."

"You do that," Isadore said. Roman watched his round, disconsolate shape disappear through the door.

Officer Swoboda, one of those who had forsaken the warehouse fight, a man counting the months to his pension, stood over Roman as he knelt beside the wrecked furniture. No attempt had been made to reassemble the antiques, just to lay corresponding pieces together. Roman could do nothing about the mutilated girl, but he could do something about this.

"Excuse me, Officer, have you got any epoxy here?"

"Yeah, but that's department property."

Roman pulled a twenty from his money clip. The guard looked at the closed door dumbly. Roman rubbed the bill between his fingers so that it crackled. Officer Swoboda's hearing proved to be his most acute sense. He fetched the tubes of epoxy and stood poised for any more errands.

Roman ignored the policeman while he cleared an adequate working space. The silver was in the best shape, a small tea service by either Coney or the Huguenot Apollos Rivoire who changed his name to Revere. The slender spout had been badly crippled by the accident but was easily reparable. It was a charming set, and it was hard to imagine any collector with the taste to own it who wouldn't come to tend to it alone.

There was no way of writing off the pair of Queen Anne side chairs no matter how badly one wanted the insurance money. They had lasted two centuries of fairly constant use because they were solidly constructed of heavy mahogany. The scratches were purely superficial. A quick inspection showed that even the drake feet were originals. On the other hand, there was little to put back together of an inlaid shelf clock. The works were displayed like a twisted skeleton through the shattered case. From the carving of the center plinth and finial, it wouldn't have been the best example of Federal Massachusetts workmanship, but it was still a shame. Roman could picture it gonging madly to its death as it tumbled over the highway.

Another fatal victim was a tambour desk. It took imagination to see what it must have looked like. A trim Hepplewhite from the shape and inlay work of a broken leg. The cherrywood veneer on the shelves was largely scraped off, and the tambour section with its delicate sliding doors had separated from the lower half of the desk from the impact of the collision. He examined the insides of the drawers, checking the joining. It was here as much as the exterior that the real craftsmanship could be found. To be a joiner two hundred years ago was to be a member of a skilled profession that looked down on carpentry as a doctor would look down on a quack. The dovetail joins had held firm with an integrity Professor Oliver would have admired.

A box contained shards of Tiffany glass. A mediocre cut-down Windsor rocker was a tepee of turnings now. The sides and bottom of a dower chest gained Roman's eye for ten minutes. It had the tulip and sunflower motif of Pilgrim Connecticut, square and innocent. Roman finished his examination with a tone of disgust. He would have liked to find something incriminating about the Pilgrims.

He looked up. Officer Swoboda was puzzling his way through the *Daily News* crossword with a well-used eraser.

"That's it?" Roman asked. "That's the lot?"

"Yup." The cop didn't look away from his work.

Roman picked his jacket off the floor. It was dirty, and he was sweaty. The stubble on his cheek was a purple shadow. It took constant care to keep himself from looking like a mugger. He was halfway out the room on his way to Isadore when he remembered the pictures.

"Wait. I saw something else. Big."

Swoboda got up to lock the door behind Roman. As he stood, a canvas dropcloth slid off his perch to the floor. His chair had been the battered top half of a highboy.

"What about that epoxy?"

Roman ignored him and dragged the rest of the dropcloth away. The whole highboy was there. In parts, but there. It was an unusual Chippendale with slender cabriole legs and ball-and-claw feet. A fanciful scroll top matched the crotch walnut veneer fronts and the engraved brass handles.

"I'll need it," Roman said.

The old dowels were broken, and the double chest would never stand up again. He didn't care. He would be the good embalmer and prepare it for its funeral. He spread milky epoxy onto a piece of the scrollwork and pressed back onto the top.

"I also need some skilled help," Roman told the guard. "If you'll just hold this here."

He rigged supports from the chairs and typewriters to hold other parts of the highboy together as he did his pasting. The target of his energy soon started retaking its shape. The highboy was a graceful chest-on-chest, New England, about 1750, made from extra-light dried walnut. There was no other way the slender legs could have held under its height. He put the bottom back on a drawer.

"It's a shame you don't love them," he could hear Oliver saying as he worked, the way the old man always talked as they repaired a cabinet together. "Think of the years and the art it took to make this."

"They're only things," he would say in return. "Things are the *gaja* disease. Not for me."

"But such a beautiful disease."

The bottom apron of the brittle walnut chest had snapped off. Roman found it in a drawer. It had a boldly scalloped shell on it, with the open claw of the foot and the high scroll the final signature of a young, experimental Goddard highboy.

"Hey, that's kind of pretty," the policeman said.

"John Goddard, Newport, Rhode Island, will be glad to hear that," Roman said. He pushed himself off the floor and straightened up. It had taken more than an hour of nonstop labor putting the highboy together, and he looked as if he'd put on his clothes straight out of the washer.

"You done? You going to leave it like this? It'll fall apart."

It seemed unlikely, but there might be the first stirrings of an appreciator in the policeman. Roman gave him the benefit of the doubt and another twenty-dollar bill.

"Just stand still. If Sergeant Isadore asks where I am, tell him I had a case of Gypsy feet," Roman said on his way out.

It was after a taxi and a shower and while he was shaving that he thought about the highboy. Since he needed three shaves a day to stay presentable, he spent a lot of time in front of a steamed mirror. He prided himself on the profitable concentration he'd developed during these periods of inactivity. The only danger was in forgetting the small scar on his neck.

There was a chance Sergeant Isadore might think he put the highboy back together for fun. Maybe. In any case, it was the only excuse he could think of for spending so much time on the double chest. From the outside everything was normal. Even the nails in the pine backing were originals, hand-wrought flattened spikes. The drawers slid out easily on deftly repaired runners, and that was the first trouble. They shouldn't have slid. The rope and padding he'd seen in the photograph should have held firm over the empty drawers all the way through the accident. Unless there were something in the drawers, something heavy rolling around and slamming against the front of the drawer until the rope broke. A sixty-pound torso would have done the job.

Inside, the drawers were spotless. The dovetails interlocked as cleanly as fingers, or they had until very recently. Now each drawer had one or two dovetails gaping, warped out of contact next to other joins that were as tight as the day they were glued. He'd seen damage like it only once before, when a girl had stuffed an antique dry sink with solidified carbon dioxide, dry ice.

Roman thought the policeman would finally catch on to the last thing he was doing, but he didn't. While Roman was fumbling with the drawers, he accidentally ran the sharp metal bevel of his ring along the wood of each drawer's sides and back. Inside the hardwood exterior of any antique the drawers were made of soft pine and gouging the wood was a common method of determining whether wormholes were twisting and genuine or straight and artificial. The wormholes did something else. Their capillary action would soak up any stain that was washed off the surface of the wood. He found what he was looking for in the last drawer. The wormholes there were clotted with a rusty deposit. Roman knew the difference between blood and an oil stain.

The razor took off the first layer of epidermis, then the second and the third, provoking a bright bud of red before he noticed that he'd run into the scar again.

7

Hoddinot Sloan's house was in the Federal style, Neo-Virginian against the Massachusetts countryside, with fluted wooden columns and cornices in white on red brick, a row of french doors opening onto a well-tended garden, all of it hidden from the road leading to Newton by a line of elms. Hoddinot Sloan also seemed in the classic Federal style. A fine nose was balanced by white eyebrows. His blue eyes seemed irritated, but the distinguished gray hair was unruffled. His thin mouth was a blend of distaste and civility.

"Will you please explain your mission again?" he asked politely as he barred the door.

"Certainly. The Metropolitan Museum is compiling a study of the best private collections of early American furniture. This is for the unlikely event of part of the museum's collection being destroyed, but you know how things are in New York. If something of this nature happens, the museum wants to know exactly where it can replace damaged articles. Naturally, your name came up. I called a few times, but your line was busy. Since I was in this part of the country, I thought I'd take a chance and drop in anyway."

Sloan looked his visitor over warily. He definitely didn't look as if he were connected with any museum. With the Mafia, more likely. Sloan had never seen such dark eyes. The pupils were so large there was almost no room for the whites. The man's complexion had an unsettling tone somewhere between chocolate and red wine. His suit bunched up over a laborer's shoulders. Not the sort of man who was interested in antiques, unless he was Armenian; that could be it. Though Armenians were only good with rugs, he believed.

"Your name?"

"Grey. Roman Grey."

It wasn't always Grey, Sloan decided.

"You have a letter or some identification?"

"Of course." Roman took an envelope from his jacket and handed it to Sloan. The first thing Sloan did when he took the letter out was to check the letterhead. It actually was from the museum, a surprise, and repeated what the man had said and asked for any cooperation. It was signed by the director of the museum's American Wing.

"Oh, come in, come in," Sloan said reluctantly. He read the letter a second time as Roman entered the foyer. The interior of the house matched its outside with cream gray moldings, a grandfather clock by Willard, a complete set of four matched side chairs, the patina of old furniture and old money. Sloan eyed his visitor apprehensively as if he expected him to seize the clock under his arm and bolt through the door.

"You know something about antiques?" Sloan asked.

"A little."

"Really," Sloan said, not bothering to hide his doubt. "You don't mind if I call the museum to check this letter, do you?"

"Please, go right ahead."

Sloan didn't usher Roman into the living room; he just motioned him in with a jerk of his gray locks. It was clear he wanted to keep an eye on the intruder. The letter went into Sloan's tweed jacket like evidence. Roman stationed himself in plain view beside the fireplace and admired the mantel's plaster carving. What did a room like this do for

Sloan, he wondered. Set him off from the rest of the world, just where he wanted to be.

Sloan redialed with some exasperation and finally slammed the phone down. "Some idiotic recording. The offices are closed, and they'll be closed all weekend."

"That's too bad, but it's always like that on Fridays. And everyone's away on vacation, you know," Roman said. He'd held his breath for only a second during Sloan's call.

"Too bad for you," Sloan said. "This will have to wait until next week at the soonest then. Besides, I am personally in no mood to have a stranger snooping around my house. If I felt like meeting people, I'd be in New York for the Armory Show this instant."

"Yes. I was rather surprised that you weren't."

Sloan hesitated, not sure whether the question was impertinent. "I would be if some moron hadn't rammed into the truck carrying my exhibit and destroyed the lot. So you'll have to excuse me."

The distinguished head jerked toward the front door. Roman looked around the room. If he didn't get in now, he never would. The phone call on Monday would finish him.

"I can understand your being upset," he said as he moved slowly to the foyer. "The more one appreciates fine antiques, the more one is hurt by their thoughtless destruction."

"Yes, yes," Sloan said impatiently.

"What I don't understand," Roman said, "is how a man of your obvious good taste could put a récamier in this room. It's like putting a grand piano on a raft. Weights down that corner of the room a little bit, don't you think?"

Sloan froze with his thin mouth open during the first part of Roman's comment. The well-groomed hair bristled. By the time Roman was finished, though, the collector's eyes were mobile and curious.

"I know what I think," Sloan said. "Perhaps you should elaborate on your odd remarks."

"Forgive me, I didn't mean to offend." Roman smiled broadly. This was the time to turn on the charm. "It simply struck me that way. But look at this marvelous

Sheraton side chair you've selected to go by the window. The airiness of the center splat carving, the reeded legs and spade feet make it look as if it could float. The New York cabinetmaker who created it might have made it for this room. And then this récamier. It may just be my prejudice, but I think that the Empire style was a mistake, the worst one Napoleon ever made. Where could a daybed get such delusions of grandeur? The styles of Egypt and Rome don't mix, and it doesn't matter how much good mahogany you waste trying. It's a shame that American furniture makers had to pass through an uninventive phase like this."

Sloan listened intently. "Very forthright of you, Mr. Grey. Since you are so interested, perhaps you'd tell me whether the paint and gilt on the récamier are original?"

Roman nodded and lowered himself to the floor. He could see Sloan raising a corner of his mouth wryly. A line of sphinxes ranged along the apron of the sofa keeping their secret to themselves. This was the part where he was supposed to run his hand over the finish and make a guess. Instead, a penknife appeared in his hand. The tip of it followed the gilt around the blocky leg of the récamier underneath. Quickly, before Sloan could have second thoughts, he gouged a tiny sliver of the gilt out, holding it as if it were on a tray while he got to his feet and then put the blade on his tongue. He closed his mouth and rolled the flake against his palate. When he was satisfied, he rubbed his tongue with a handkerchief.

"It's the original, but it's not gilt. To begin with, it's a Boston récamier, and Boston furniture makers always were restrained in their use of gold, so I had my doubts. No, it's orpiment. Lovely yellow, but it hasn't been used for some time because it's poisonous, a sulfide of arsenic. Lasted as well as it has because it's in Venice turpentine. Since the orpiment is original, I think we can assume that the paint underneath is also."

"Amazing," Sloan said, genuinely impressed. His estimate of his visitor was going through some rapid changes. "It took me a week to come to that conclusion. A friend left it for an opinion, and this reaffirms what I thought. And what you said about the Empire period, I quite agree with. Napoleon was a nasty man, and he inspired a nasty style. Amazing, though. I never saw that done before. Have you been poisoned by any chance?"

Roman smiled. Sloan was a good deal warmer than he had been before. "No. I would appreciate some water to wash my mouth out, however."

"Naturally, naturally," Sloan said. "While I get it for you, let me show you to the rose garden. There are a couple Houdon bathers there you might enjoy. This way."

The rose garden was on the other side of the house, the shady side so that the flowers could last out the summer. Roman eased himself into an iron chair facing the marble bathers and thinking about Hoddinot Sloan. If the fish was not on the hook, he was very interested in the bait.

"Here we are." Sloan emerged from a door farther down the house at what must have been the kitchen. He was bearing a salver with a bottle of white wine and two glasses. "Might as well wash our mouths with a good year." He set the tray down on the table between them. "What do you think of the bathers?"

"Much more attractive than Madame Récamier."

Sloan laughed. Real teeth, Roman noted. For a man in his late fifties Sloan kept himself up as well as his house.

"That was quite a trick. Where did you pick it up?" Sloan asked. It was meant to sound like a cross between curiosity and congratulations instead of envy.

"Simply an old method," Roman told him. "The difficulty is in differentiating from the other sulfides used in painting. Of course, arsenic has a definite taste of its own. Excuse me." He spit a mouthful of Vouvray onto the grass.

"Bitter almonds, isn't it?" Sloan said.

Roman nodded. "Something like that. How did you know?"

"Mystery books. I must read a hundred a year," Sloan confessed with a touch of pride. "I just wish some of them were harder to figure out. But about this problem with the sulfides, are there any other ways of finding out which is which?"

"Oh, yes. Putting a sample into a spoon and holding a match underneath is one way. The smells are often quite characteristic. And as a last resort, you can burn it. I'm sure you can read a flame for pigments or zinc."

Sloan smiled reassuringly while his eyes betrayed ignorance. The two men were equals now, even friends, until Sloan could appropriate the odd visitor's knowledge. The remark that it was simply an "old method" was too vague for him to accept.

"You collect yourself," the host prompted.

"Study. I'm afraid I don't have the money to surround myself with beauty the way you have, so I content myself with scholarship. From time to time, I advise beginning collectors."

Sloan gave another of his smiles of understanding. There were so many people trying to buy their way into society with the purchase of a Chippendale chair or two, usually at inflated prices. His visitor was getting more and more interesting.

"I'm sorry," Roman said. "Here I am taking up all your time when I was about to go. Thanks very much for the wine; the Loire grapes are my favorite. Now I will be on my way. It's a long drive back to the city."

"Wait," Sloan said as if something had just occurred to him, although he'd been thinking about it for the past minute. "Have you got a room in Boston?"

"No," Roman admitted. "I just dropped by today because this is my last week with the museum. They'll be sending someone else out next week."

That was enough for Sloan.

"Then I insist. You must stay here for the weekend. The director is an old friend of mine, and the least I can do is cooperate, and I'd find it a pleasure to show the collection to someone I know would appreciate it. I'll have the guest room readied. The servants will bring your luggage from your car. You have no other plans for the weekend?"

It was more an order than a question, but Roman displayed the decent amount of hesitation.

Sloan winked. "She'll wait. They always do." It was meant as a masculine insight, though it had that inevitable element of upper-class fantasy for the sexual life of "other types." How many times had Roman run into that myth when he was on the road with a *kumpania*, the *gaja* gaping on the sides of the road, nudging each other and not bothering to whisper about the Gypsy girls with their precocious breasts and bright petticoats—"The darker the cherry, the sweeter the meat"—totally unaware and probably not caring that there was no female more chaste than a Gypsy? The girl who gave away her virginity gave away her seat by the Romany fire.

"Okay," Roman said. "If you'd really like me to."

After another glass, a maid came and showed Roman to his room. His suitcase was already in it, opened on the bed, and his toilet kit was in the bathroom. He washed under his arms and shaved and laid himself out over the bed. The whole thing would have been easier to reconstruct if he'd been Isadore. He stared blankly at the dun-colored ceiling, so tastefully in place with the Georgian decor of the room. Nanoosh. A Chippendale highboy. A body in several parts, making a murder out of an accident. A funeral with Madame Vera.

Hoddinot Sloan. A man very interested and fairly knowledgeable about antiques. Wealthy, from what? The murder of whales, slaving, rum? It didn't matter; money, it was universally acknowledged, got a polish with age. A snob, a man who found it difficult to deal with people. The tweed jacket and the lemon turtleneck, the banker's profile, the signet ring with the crest were just more furniture to surround himself with. A possessive man, a man who should have gone to New York outraged at the loss of the van's delicate cargo. An ultimate *gajo*, who for some reason was not acting like one.

What had he said? That he was not in the mood for meeting people. Sloan wasn't the sort of man who stayed home to be alone with his thoughts. He was expecting something. Not someone, or he would never have invited a stranger to stay. The ploy with the récamier was barely enough to secure an invitation as it was. Sloan's greed had swung it. It wasn't strong enough to get him out, to go down to New York, but it was enough to have a stranger in his house for some information on the free. An unpleasant man, Hoddinot Sloan.

A maid knocked on the door to report that dinner was being served. Roman dug a fresh shirt out of his suitcase, put it on and topped it with a tie.

8

"There you are," Sloan said with an air of discovery as Roman entered the dining room.

There were three places set at the table, Royal Worcester on San Dominican mahogany. The dining room was similar to the others Roman had seen with the addition of a patriotic wooden eagle.

Sloan removed a bottle of white wine that had been perspiring in a silver basket and filled their glasses. As a bit of before-dinner conversation, he asked Roman whether he could identify the various pieces in the room. It was a simple, tedious task, but Roman did it with a smile. After all, what else could Sloan imagine that they had in common? Loving? Hating? A slaughtered girl? It was an intimation of Roman's social standing that Sloan didn't bother to suggest who the third diner might be until she appeared.

"Oh Hillary, we were wondering where you were. This is Mr. Grey; he's staying over for the weekend. My daughter."

Hillary had a cool hand, like the glass of wine. Roman had seen her picture in the living room in a frame from

49

Biddle, Banks and Bailey. As she sat down, she still seemed to be in a sterling silver frame. Her hair was long and so fair as almost to be white. She'd inherited her father's eyes of ice blue and a full mouth from someone else. She was dressed in a chic blouse, pants and an embroidered leather vest. Roman guessed her age at nineteen.

"Something new," she said as a greeting.

"I'm glad to meet you, too," Roman said. Before she could take umbrage, he gave her a wide smile of brilliant teeth against his dark face.

She looked from Roman to her father trying to figure out the connection. "Well, Father, I thought I knew all your friends."

Sloan blushed. "Mr. Grey is here to compile a list of the collection for the Metropolitan Museum."

"Ah." It was neat and informative. She'd not only put her father down with an ease that showed practice but also put the visitor in his place. There was an embarrassed pause while she innocently smoothed her napkin over her lap.

"Let's eat," her father said suddenly, as if it were a good idea.

The supper was an overcooked scrod and a salad, the sort of meal designed for a middle-aged man watching his weight. Roman grew sympathetic to Sloan's digestion as the girl led the conversation from one sore subject to another in a soft, sweet voice. She was like a surgeon probing with a scalpel not to dispel pain but create it.

"My father's a very good collector. I'm so happy your museum is becoming aware of that fact. I bet there's not another man in Boston with his eye for value. Remember the time"—she turned for aid from her father—"when that old Irishwoman asked you to look at that chest. You know, she'd been a maid to one of the Cabot families her whole life, and all she got out of it was a dirty old bureau. She was practically in rags, you told me. Anyway, Father took one look at it and knew it was a, what, a William and Mary, that's right. He paid her fifty dollars for it, brought it here and cleaned it, and sold it two months later for three thousand dollars."

She slid a fish knife down the flaccid spine of the scrod.

"My friends are all against the war. I mean, half of

them are in Canada, and the rest are trying to break a toe or something before their physical rather than let themselves be turned into cannon fodder. So far as I'm concerned that's a lot braver than just letting yourself be inducted. The silly boys aren't as original as they think, though. Father was just as smart as they are now and it was a lot more unpopular in World War II. It took real nerve claiming a bad back then, don't you think?"

By the time she was finished she'd picked her father as clean as the fish. Sloan's eyes had the watery look of a man who was knocked out and merely refused to fall. The unusual aspect in the girl's attack, what made it so effective, was an absence of any feeling. She didn't act from betrayal or pique the way a daughter should. It reminded him of the absent presence in the framed pictures. There were no photos of her mother in the house. The ones of Sloan and the girl together belied the idea that he ever held her on his lap for anything but portraits. He was the sort of father who sent his daughter from one boarding school to another, probably showing up late if at all on Father's Day and then making contact with the other fathers instead of with Hillary Sloan. Now he was paying for it.

She wasn't just a girl anymore. Roman could feel her physical presence, the line that led down her cheek to a stylishly long neck to the casually unbuttoned blouse and the fact that no bra restrained her breasts as she twisted back and forth from her father to the fish. At the same time he was aware that she was studying him. It was unusual enough for a man like him to be sitting across from her whether he was from the museum or not. The few electric shocks she directed at him—"I've always supposed that immigrants understood better how bestial this country is"—got no reaction, and this mystified her further.

Roman began feeling sordid for having insinuated himself into the Sloan household to hear a dinner conversation that, except for its degree, was taking place in a million other American homes at the same time. He had to remind himself that it was necessary. The *vilos*, the old witches of Rumania, could work magic on a person only when they had something of his, a fingernail, a hair. Something to make him concrete. Roman didn't depend on magic, but he understood the truth of the system. He needed the frigid, arrogant pulse of the Sloans, or else he would be blind the way he had been on the highway trying to decipher a stretch of road and a handful of photographs. He was no detective. This was the only way he could work, the way the Romany had always worked.

Hillary was talking about a rock festival. Sloan listened with a frown of disapproval. As she spoke, she raised her arms above her head, the imprint of her nipples through her blouse adding another level of intimidation. Sloan looked outside.

Roman watched with interest. Few *gaja* understood the physical language between people, and the girl herself probably didn't know what a good job she was doing of undermining her father. When her luxurious stretch was done and she saw that Roman had not diverted his eyes to his lettuce, she stared straight at him. His eyes still didn't fall.

"That's a beautiful vest," Roman commented. "Kid leather had a religious significance during the Middle Ages. Especially black kid."

"Oh, she has one of those, too," Sloan said, eager to tell what he had given her.

"Really? You're an expert on any number of things," Hillary said. He watched the pupils of her blue eyes narrow with dislike. "I guess that's a lesson. Those who can't afford things know the most about them."

"I'm afraid that's the truth." Roman smiled disarmingly.

The dessert came, glass bowls of sherbet. Sloan took small, disheartened scoops of his. His daughter took one large spoonful, praised it extravagantly, and let the lemon-colored ice melt into a puddle of conspicuous consumption. Roman enjoyed his completely.

"Have you got reservations up in the White Mountains?" Sloan asked. It was a last attempt to establish his role as patriarch.

"Reservations at a rock festival would be a little illogical, Father," Hillary said, as if she were explaining affairs to a slow child. Her nostrils dilated, and her fingers rose a quarter inch from the table.

"Cigarette?" Roman asked. His hand held out his pack of Gauloises to her. Because that was what she had been thinking of and what her minute gestures told Roman, she took it before she could stop herself. "They're strong things, but they're all I have," he said.

To give back the cigarette would be a confession of weakness. Hillary accepted his light.

"*Très chic,*" she said with a motion of the Gauloise.

"*Très* cheap," Roman told her.

Sloan attempted to drag the conversation back to the festival. His daughter led him on effortlessly. There had been a change in the relationship between the girl and the visitor. She showed off for Roman. He sat back and watched them, taking in the polite Sloan ferocity, their Royal Worcester, their inlaid mahogany prosperity, their worm-eaten ancestry, their hair and fingernails.

As an exercise in imagination, he placed a dismembered body on the table in between the father and daughter and tried to see if it fit.

9

It wasn't a good night for sleeping. The bed was made of pillows, and the Sloans spun around a lightless antique shop. He couldn't make out what they said. Finally, he slept on the floor.

Breakfast was Continental, croissants and coffee. He had that to be thankful for. The cook made his pot double strength, and he poured a stream of sugar into it. It was before eight, and only he and the staff were up. When he was finished, he went out into the garden.

Sloan's taste for things Virginian showed in the landscaping. No native evergreens were allowed to intrude, and the few maples were barely tolerated. The garden with the marble bathers was divided from the rose garden by a trellis. There was a second trellis halfway down the side of the lawn serving as camouflage for a potting shed. He wandered down to it and found nothing more suspicious than varmint poison. Rather than come back through the yard he crossed to the Sloan driveway. A yellow Buick station wagon was parked in it. He followed the driveway to the front of the house. On the west end were two rooms he had not yet seen, an office and a workroom with neat rows of paint cans and, hung on hooks from the walls, legs and arms salvaged from discarded possessions.

"Looking for something?"

Hillary came around from the gardens. She was in a green one-piece riding outfit with jodhpur wings and high boots. Her hands were on her hips. The effect of the green and her white-gold hair was what she wanted it to be.

"Yes, you," Roman said. "The house is lovely, but I was hoping for some company. Maybe I'm just an early riser."

"Maybe," Hillary said, but didn't bother keeping up the tension. "I can't say that I like it. We used to have a house in Cambridge. When my mother died, we sold it. The neighborhood was changing, Father said. We bought this. I still don't like it."

"How long ago was that?"

"Twelve years. Before I forget, he sent me to fetch you. He's at the breakfast table."

Hoddinot Sloan appeared to have recovered from last night's dinner. He dabbed half a croissant with marmalade as he welcomed Roman.

"Sleep well? That's a pencil post four-poster in your room, you know."

"I'm sure he does," Hillary commented. She poured twin braids of milk and coffee into her cup.

"Which is more than I can say for you." Her father went on. "I've tried to interest Hillary in the study of antiques for years. All she can think of is horses and hippies, a fairly individual combination but not one likely to stimulate the brain."

Far away at the rear of the lawn a gardener laid out sprinklers. When they stretched from one fence to the other, he bent down to a water nozzle hidden in the grass and turned it on. A series of rooster tails erupted from the grass. The works, Roman thought, had also been turned on beneath Sloan's own manicured exterior. Last night's dinner had not been a normal one; he wasn't a man to invite an audience to his own execution.

"Father disapproves," she said. She crossed her arms, drawing the knit riding suit tight around her chest. Sloan still didn't know how to handle the outlined maturity of her body. Sex, as usual, was the ultimate weapon. "Do you jump?" she asked Roman.

"Occasionally. On hot sand, things of that sort."

"No, no, jump horses. That's Hillary's hobby," Sloan said.

Hillary giggled. "I thought it was quite funny." She began laughing again. The happier she was, the younger she looked.

"Ridiculous," Sloan said. The last shred of croissant vanished into his mouth. "Come on, Grey. We have a lot of work to do."

While Hillary went down a path to the stables, Sloan escorted Roman into his private office. Sloan had chosen second-rate antiques for the room, good enough to lend a pleasant air but nothing whose value would be ruined by wear.

"Very wise," Roman said. "A lot of people would have just put these into storage."

Sloan pointed to the files. "I never waste anything. I got these at a dollar apiece. Simply replaced the runners and cemented strips on the drawers, and they're good as new. I've been offered a hundred apiece for them now. Tell me, how do you plan to categorize the collection?"

Roman explained that he intended no comprehensive catalogue, just a detailed list of those pieces that were of exhibition value. Sloan volunteered that he had photos of every piece that went through his hands with records of any restoration that had been done to them.

"It's a matter of protection," he added. "I don't want anyone accusing me of bad faith. I tell them exactly what they're buying. I may not tell people what they have when they're selling to me; that's part of the game. Otherwise, they shouldn't be in it."

Roman nodded obediently, and Sloan went on.

"I'll tell you this, no one can accuse me of shady practices like so many New York collectors."

"Are there many people like, uh, that in Boston?"

Sloan sniffed. "Mostly Irish here. I thought it was a good time to leave the city when the Kennedys bought it."

Sloan's bigotry rose like a whale through the calm surface of a sea. It blew off its supply of bile and in a few moments returned to the depths of his personality. The conversation moved back to antiques.

"It must have made you very sad when your Armory

shipment was destroyed. Perhaps it wasn't total," Roman
suggested. "If you could restore the files and you have
photos, you might be able to restore some of those pieces."

Sloan shrugged the suggestion off. "I doubt it.
Besides—you'll find this hard to believe—they're being
held as evidence or something by the New York police.
Some murder or a body, I haven't got it straight."

Roman raised his eyebrows with wonder.

"It is presumptuous, I agree," Sloan said. "But apparently the man who ran into the van was hiding a dead
girl in his car. If it hadn't been for the accident, he probably would have gotten away with the crime."

"Didn't the police tell you anything more?"

"No." Sloan sighed. "An affair of passion most likely.
That's what these cases usually are. Emotional things."

Sloan opened his desk and took out four loose-leaf fold-
ers. The pages were full of notes and snapshots. He gave
them to Roman to carry as they moved to his workshop.
A sharp blend of turpentine and sawdust permeated the
room. Dowels of varying thicknesses stood in an ascending
line like the pipes of an organ. A large rotary saw stood
on one side. On the walls were the dismantled trophies Roman had seen through the window, cabriole and reeded
legs with ball-and-claw, hair paw, pad and spade feet. A
bright fluorescent light in the shape of a halo hung from
the ceiling.

Roman put the notebooks down and took out his own
notebook and pen. Sloan dragged a dropcloth off a small
serving table. It was New England Sheraton rather than
Philadelphian, from about 1800. At any auction it would
draw a very good price and Roman had to admit it was
museum class.

"I purchased this for, let's say five thousand. I'll sell it
for much more," Sloan told him. "Can you tell me how I
was able to buy it for so little? Also, can you tell me
where you have seen work by the same artist here?"

Sloan was insatiable. A mania for tests was in the best
of *gaja*, and it was something that Roman could never
comprehend, an "it's how you perform today that counts"
attitude that explained their frustration with sex. Served
them right. Roman ran his hand along the fine carving of

the legs and the glossy mahogany of the drawer fronts. He didn't have the patience to keep Sloan in suspense.

"Samuel McIntire did the carving, and you can see the design is basically the same as the mantel in your living room. I admired it the first day I was here. That puts us in Salem. McIntire didn't do the lid on this top, however; that's the trademark of William Hood. They collaborated on this piece. How did you get the bargain?"

He opened the drawers. Except for lathing on the bottom of the sides to correct a droop, they were the originals.

"The back. The back was broken in," Roman said.

Sloan's mouth dropped as far as it decently could.

"How did you know that? You haven't even pulled the table away from the wall to see the back."

If it had been yesterday when he needed to impress Sloan, Roman would have answered with some dramatics. Today he was a bored magician.

"I'm afraid that's all it could have been. Obviously everything else is in perfect condition. Besides, a few of the old traditions persisted in Salem into the nineteenth century. The witchcraft trials, you know, and some of the old fears. It wasn't rare for a descendant of one of the accused ladies to have his house and all his furniture broken in some way after he died. It was supposed to ruin any hiding place that his spirit might try to reside in. Being thrifty New Englanders, they usually chose to do the damage someplace where it wouldn't show. They must have been a strange people."

"Indeed," Sloan agreed. He pulled the table out. A new pine panel covered the back. "To think that a ghost would hide away in a table."

"A highboy would be more comfortable, wouldn't it?"

Confusion clouded Sloan's face and then passed.

"Oh, yes. I see what you mean. Much more comfortable." He laughed. "Anyway, as you no doubt suspect, I'll stain the pine to match the rest of the table."

"You'll use handwrought nails."

"Naturally. Look, they're in. Tight as a coffin."

The serving table filled the first page of Roman's notebook. There were others to come from Sloan's collection, and both men had worked up an appetite by lunchtime.

10

Lunch was a *salade Niçoise* and a bottle of Tavel. The delicate fare was starting to make Roman's stomach growl in disdain. Sloan directed the conversation to the fictitious collectors whom Roman advised.

"Without naming names, of course," Sloan said. "I understand the discretion involved. Even with *nouveau riche.* You use only New York dealers?"

Roman said that wasn't necessarily true. It was enough encouragement to keep Sloan talking until Roman's salad bowl was empty.

"Starving, aren't you?" Hillary asked.

Sloan's face turned red. "Get those animals out of here. I've told you a million times about those horses. The gardener hasn't got time to clean up after them."

Hillary looked down and smiled. She was seated on a bay Morgan, and she held the reins of a second horse in her free hand. She was a good enough horsewoman to have crept up silently with the two. It was when she was arrogant that she was most her father's daughter, and then both of them seemed to be set in clear plastic.

"I'll get them off the lawn on one condition. Mr. Grey

comes with me. He could use some exercise after being cooped up all morning with old chairs and tables."

"Mr. Grey has a job to do. There are a number of things, porcelain glass that he has yet to see."

Hillary slouched in her saddle. "I can wait."

Sloan's hand, the one with the signet ring, ran through his silver hair. He looked back and forth from his daughter to Roman, who assumed a pose of complete impartiality.

"You don't want him to see too much, do you, Father? He might get tired. Some riding in the open air might freshen him up."

Sloan lost some color in his cheeks.

"Well, how about it?" he asked Roman with the little grace he could muster.

"I think you'll have a surplus of fertilizer unless I do." Roman laughed. He approached his horse, a handsome bay with a star, and patted his neck. He always liked the hot sheen the coat of a good horse had.

"Okay." Sloan gave in. "A short ride. I'll expect you back in an hour."

"By the way," Roman said, "if you feel like it, you might want to set up some paints. We can discuss different methods of analysis when I return."

Hillary led the way off the lawn on her horse while Roman walked his. When he felt they were out of eyesight, he swung onto the horse's back. They waited until a truck went by on the highway and crossed. A dirt road led to a stable and corral. They took another one into the woods.

"What are you here for?" she asked.

"What?"

"You heard me. What do you want? Why are you getting so friendly with my father?"

She ducked under a branch as if it were an insult hardly worth noticing.

"I'm making a list of antiques. Collectors who cooperate find me full of charm."

She looked at him shrewdly through golden lashes. "You claim to be a psychologist then."

"No. You learn how to deal with people in my profession."

"Oh, come on. I'm not as dumb as my father. I'd say if

a man like you didn't want something really badly from my father, you'd just blow him and his whole house down. I see you more around nightclubs or lions than a collection of antiques."

They came through a copse of trees to a meadow. The high grass steamed with insects in the afternoon sun. A thrush moved over the field in short dashes. Roman's knees clamped the sides of the horse comfortably, though he would have preferred to do without the saddle.

"It's true I get violent over antimacassars," Roman confessed, slapping his horse's neck. "What's his name?"

Hillary tilted her head to look at him. "You're changing the subject." After a minute of silent riding, a genuine smile edged onto her lips. "His name's Blaze. Not very original, is it?"

"And yours?"

"Brownie. They're good horses all the same," she said proudly. The grasshoppers wildly evacuated their path as she scrutinized her riding partner. "Questions now, Mr. Grey? Something innocent first and then lead up to the biggies? But I can't ask you questions, like what brings you into the bosom of the nation's dullest family?"

"I give up." Roman sighed. "I came for the secret of your scrod with mock cream sauce. If I can't get that, I'll settle for the *salade Niçoise* made with Velveeta."

"Seriously. I can't get it out of my mind why someone like you is interested in my father. Has he got himself involved in something?"

Roman looked around. The girl's questions were almost lost in the din of the insects. It wasn't the noise that made the hair on the back of his neck stand up but the feeling that they weren't alone.

"You think your father's done something wrong?"

"Another question is not an answer." Tiny beads of sweat appeared at her hairline. The sun had lacquered Roman copper. "I happen to know you're from the police." She paused. "Or the Mafia."

Roman slapped his hand over his face. She flushed and rode on with her jaw set firmly. He took his hand off his face to wipe the tears away, and she saw her suspicions were correct. He had been laughing. "God, I can't wait until I see Isadore," he said. "The Mafia, what'll be next?"

"Very funny," Hillary agreed grimly. "So you're just a poor man interested in antiques and mixing with the upper crust. You must ride pretty well then."

He was still wiping his eyes when Hillary stopped Brownie beside a raspberry bush and fed him some of the berries. Blaze nuzzled her hand until she gave some to him as well. They'd gone on another ten yards when Blaze's ears perked up. He reared, stamping his two rear legs. The horse twisted the reins out of Roman's hands and looked back, the pink sides of his eyes showing. The stirrups swung into his legs like ballpeen hammers. Roman caught one blurred look at Hillary's satisfied beam before the horse bolted.

Blaze was a strong young Morgan sixteen hands high, and he was going at top speed when he crashed into the woods. Roman simply tried to stay on. It was impossible to see through the branches that tried to pull him off. Suddenly the horse stumbled. Roman slid to one side just as the horse ended his fall against a tree, crushing his rider between himself and the trunk. Blaze regained his footing and plunged forward. Both of Roman's hands were tangled in the Morgan's mane. He was still on, but his chest refused to expand. There was a dark edge to his vision of the approaching trees. He batted his eyes trying to clear them. He felt the horse starting down an incline before he saw it.

The underbrush became sparser as Blaze slid down the incline regaining velocity, and the black ring closed in on Roman's sight. He could make out a stone fence at the bottom of the bank. The horse would never make the jump with him hanging on like a sack of cement. A shriek that wasn't his own reverberated in his ears. Blaze's flanks bunched in response to his training as they reached the end of the bank and the fence. There was no edge of Roman's vision now, just total darkness.

As Blaze coiled, Roman rose on his knees. There was little point in hesitating. He turned his heels in, squeezed them hard, and rolled all his weight forward onto the horse's withers. He called "Jump," blindly and Blaze answered, throwing his sixteen hundred pounds into the air. The surge carried Roman weightlessly up, and he heard two sharp clicks, the sounds of Blaze's front hooves grazing the edge of the wall.

Roman flattened himself against the horse's powerful muscles as it landed and came to a halt. When he straightened up, the knot that had been around his throat was off. He could make out lights and shadows. While the jumper stood and shook with fright, Roman spoke to him and smoothed the febrile trembling in his neck.

Roman turned at the sound of a second horse coming down the bank. He could clearly see Hillary bringing Brownie expertly over the fence. She rode up looking very scared. Blaze shied when she joined them.

"Oh, Mr. Grey, I—"

"I know," Roman said. He slid off the horse to his feet and approached Blaze's head, patting him all the way. One dark hand rubbed Blaze's star, and the other delicately searched his nostrils until he brought out a tiny sprig. He sniffed it. "Rosemary, right? It would pep up the dullest horse, let alone a healthy one."

He took the horse by the reins and walked him to let him cool. Hillary got off Brownie and walked by his side. Her lips were tight, and he could almost hear her trying to think of something to say. He didn't know what he wanted to say. She seemed authentically frightened now, but there was a point in the woods when she could have caught up and helped. He didn't even hear her until he was going down the bank.

"I just wanted to scare you."

"Weren't you afraid I'd sic my mob on you?" he asked sardonically.

"I guess I made a mistake."

"I'd call it a tantrum. And now I'm throwing a tantrum." A noise of disgust came out of his throat. "Maybe this will teach me not to go riding with flirts on horses named Blaze."

He sat down where he was under a tree.

Roman struggled to stifle a painful laugh of rue. Hillary sat down with him and stared. The horses wandered deeper into the shade of the tree, a large old oak.

"I almost get you killed and you think it's funny. You are the strangest person I've ever met," she said.

"You lead a sheltered life." He stuck a blade of grass in

his mouth. His jacket was torn, but it was plain he wasn't losing any blood.

"Now I know you're not here just to look at Daddy's antiques."

Roman frowned. "Daddy? I thought it was something more formal, like Father or *Pater*."

"In moments of stress I revert," she confessed. "Not often, I guarantee you."

"I'll take your word." He rejected the blade and chose another. "You've got him on the run with that threat about me seeing too much. What is it, phony labels?"

Hillary picked a blade of grass for herself.

"I saw the paper through the window this morning," Roman went on, "and I saw the ink when I went into the workshop with your father."

She took the blade from her mouth and tossed it like a tiny green spear. "Isn't he the phony? Christ! If he'd been on Blaze, he would have fainted. And if he'd caught me afterward, he would have killed me."

"You're kidding, aren't you?"

"Oh, I don't know."

"What about your mother?" He thought she might react with her police suspicions. She simply shook her head.

"No mother, not even a picture anymore. She had 'bad blood,' according to my father, who is the one person in the twentieth century who still uses that phrase. The truth is she was coming home from a charity ball one night and she drove the car into the Charles River, taking her lover with her. Now, when I come home at four in the morning, which is usual whenever I'm at home, my father tells me that I have 'bad blood.' I haven't got a generation gap with him, I've got a historical gap."

She drew the pack of Gauloises from his shirt pocket and lit one for each of them. As Roman accepted the cigarette in his mouth, his eyes half shut, she studied him. The bridge of his nose was sharp enough for a knife, and his skin looked as if it had been patiently oiled by a tanner. Instead of being trim, his waist was a solid continuation of his barrel chest, and yet, in all, there was something uniquely appealing about the combination.

"That language you were speaking to Blaze when I came up. It was Gypsy, wasn't it?" she said softly.

Roman was surprised. "How did you know?"

"A teacher introduced me to some once in Switzerland. So your name isn't really Grey, is it?"

"Yes. Not the color gray; there isn't such a color to Gypsies. The closest translation would be 'horse,' actually."

"Oh," Hillary said in a chastened voice. "Many famous Gypsy jockeys?"

" 'Jockey' is a Gypsy word."

They nodded at each other, compressing smiles on their lips.

"Give me some other words," she said. "I'm interested."

"Okay." He looked up at the underbellies of the leaves. "Since you seek enlightenment, a *camo djili:*

> *Pawnie birks*
> My *men-engri* shall be;
> *Yackors* my dudes
> Like *ruppeny* shine:
> *Atch meery chi,*
> *Ma jal* away,
> Perhaps I may not *dick tute*
> *Kek komi.*

His voice was husky, conversational, but there was an energy in it she hadn't heard before. Hillary was suddenly aware that the strange language he was speaking was his first tongue, the one he thought in.

"I liked it. What was it?" she asked.

"A love song. It goes, in a slightly bowdlerized version:

> I'd choose as pillows for my head
> Those snow-white breasts of thine.
> I'd use as lamps to light my bed
> Those eyes of silver shine.
> O lovely maid, disdain me not,
> Nor leave me in my pain,
> Perhaps 'twill never be my lot
> To see thy face again.

Hillary was more affected than he'd expected. She turned away and stubbed her cigarette out on the ground.

"What's the matter?" he asked.

"That's pretty trite stuff," she said brutally.

"Gypsies are pretty simple people," Roman said, taken aback. "You're a modern, sophisticated girl. A Gypsy isn't. A friend of mine has been telling me all about primitive insects found in amber. That's what Gypsies are. Anachronisms, throwbacks. Living fossils, and they don't know. Appreciate them while you can." He didn't like lecturing; but he liked her now, and he wanted to get through.

"Now you're being trite. Come on, my father is waiting for you."

He raised his eyebrows in surprise. Blaze whinnied amiably as they approached. At least someone had a sentimental soul, Roman told himself. Hillary looked in every direction but his.

They were riding back through the field where Blaze had bolted when Hillary put her hand on Roman's thigh.

"The song was fine. Really. We can stop here if you like."

She'd already reined Brownie to a halt, and he stopped Blaze.

"Don't worry. You didn't hurt my feelings."

"I'd like to, very much. Wouldn't you?" she asked.

She was sincere. Her blue eyes held his frankly. The golden body that rode so lightly would be very real and pleasant under him.

"Yes, I would. But I won't."

He dug his heels into Blaze's sides, disrupting the kingdom of the grasshoppers, leaving before he changed his mind.

11

The room was in dark except for one flame, a fat verdigris glow that lit only the nostrils, cheeks and brows of the two men so that they looked like nothing more than grotesque levitating masks. The strong stench of rotten eggs permeated the room.

"It all depends on the amount of zinc," Roman said. "That and whether you use earth pigments or chemical compounds."

"This is safer than tasting?" Sloan asked.

"Not as a steady atmosphere. On the other hand, sulfur and lead won't do your stomach any good."

Sloan squinted into the fumes of the flame he held in the teaspoon. Roman turned aside to breathe. They had been burning paints in Sloan's workshop for two hours. He had to give the man credit: Sloan was a fast learner.

"You can make the pigments also?" Sloan asked.

"Sure, if you want to take the trouble. Buying it in the store is simpler and cheaper."

"Naturally, naturally," Sloan agreed. "But I'm restoring the récamier. I'm not going to be able to buy orpiment in any store, am I?"

"No," Roman admitted.

"Well then, how difficult is it to make? I'll have to have some."

"Not difficult at all."

"How?"

Roman felt one heartbeat pass through his chest like a train in the dark. There was no way to avoid an answer.

"Simple. All you need is sulfur, arsenic and a covered crucible. Heat it and let it cool. The orpiment will gather on the cover."

"That's it?"

"Yes. And don't mix it with lead or copper carbonate because neither will go with a sulfide. And don't taste it."

"It's that powerful?" Sloan urged.

"You wouldn't be able to poison anybody with it," Roman said lightly. "It would be impossible to disguise the taste. Some artists have died, though, without wanting to."

Sloan blew the flame out, and the room was black for a moment until Roman put the light on. The dealer was not trying to hide his satisfaction. He'd learned more in one afternoon than he had in a year. The future unfolded as a calendar of profits in his mind. Roman opened the door and stepped into the office. The stink of sulfur had insinuated itself there, too, and he went on to the living room without waiting for his host.

"I suppose you're hungry," Sloan said when he caught up.

Dinner was a cold salmon. Roman paid more attention to the brandy. He'd had his fill of the *gaja* household and its diet. What he wanted now was a hot stew bright with paprika with the loud arguing of hungry Romanies, not gelid civility. He withdrew into himself as Hillary tried to gain his attention with her wit. If he had pumped the father and daughter dry, they had pumped him, too. Sloan attempted to draw him into a dispute over the merits of the Reveres and got nothing but grunts. It didn't matter to Sloan. He would be rid of his guest tomorrow, and he had what he wanted.

Roman retired early, going to his room and making a bed for himself on the floor. He put an ashtray beside him and smoked one Gauloise after another in the dark. Below he could hear them still carrying on. Sloan wanted to

know what she and the Armenian had been doing in the
woods for so long. She said he wasn't Armenian, and who
was her father to talk about fooling around? He said he
didn't care what Grey was; he wanted her to stay away
from him. They weren't yelling. From the tone of their
voices, a conversational hum, many people wouldn't have
been aware that they were arguing. But it was far hotter
than any talk Roman had heard between them before. The
strain of living together for even a short time was beginning to split their charade at the seam. The wooden beams
of the old house carried their mutual hate like a wire
transmitting electricity.

She excused herself and left to drive to Boston to see
some friends. Sloan said good-night and reminded her that
she knew what he'd do if any of her friends showed up
around his house. Roman expected Sloan to go to his bedroom soon after that, but instead he moved to his office.
The sounds of drawers opening and feet pacing went on
for two hours. At last, Sloan slammed the office door shut,
locked it, and went upstairs to bed. Roman waited another
hour for his host to fall asleep.

He got up and opened a window that looked out over
the back lawn. The stars were very bright, dimming only
where they came close to the nearly full moon. Scorpio
sprawled up from the trees. Cassiopeia, the Queen of Ethi-
opia, reigned over the duller subjects. Roman's cigarette
imitated a shooting star as it spun out the window to the
grass.

No gardener on a night shift appeared. Roman sat on
the sill with his stockinged feet hanging over the two-story
drop to the lawn. He let go and came down on the grass
on all fours. He had a moment of fear when he lost his
breath, but it returned as he moved back into the shadow
of the house. The last thing he wanted was to be staggering about blind and gagging outside a locked house.

He was in the garden where Sloan had first offered him
a glass of wine. The marble bathers held each other for
warmth under the moon. He moved around the trellis to
the rose garden and past to where the house spread to ac-
commodate Sloan's workshop and office. Roman stopped
in front of the image of himself in Sloan's office.

Sloan's arrogance showed in the precautions he took

against theft. There was no electric alarm system, just two impressively heavy bolts on the sides of the window. During the time Roman spent in the office while Sloan sorted out paints and spoons, he'd had ample time to remove the latch screws. The sturdy bolts were shot and secure, but Roman lifted the window easily, the bar carrying the latch with it.

Roman passed through the office into the workshop. Because Sloan kept his silver there, he'd kept a closer eye on Roman in this room. The paints were still out, and sulfur clung to the air. He picked out the saw with his pocket flashlight. It was a relatively new machine, large enough to split a tree with, no doubt an instrument of pride to its owner. A ring of curling teeth rested in the thin slot. Roman took the saw out of gear and turned the wheel slowly in the light's beam. There was no sign of blood. The teeth had been cleaned very recently.

He turned the light onto the floor. The sawdust was new, and there were no stains under it that he could see. He crouched next to the wheel and examined the slot it lay in. The cleaning hadn't been as thorough here. The back end of the groove was spotted brown. It would take sawing a board dripping with stain to produce them, if it were stain.

In another half hour there was nothing else to find in the shop besides the metal stamps Sloan did his forging with. A sample read: "Mills & Deming, 374 Queen ſtreet, two doors above the Friends Meeting, NEW YORK, Makes and ſells, all kinds of Cabinet Furniture and Chairs, after the moſt modern faſhions and on reaſonable terms." Mills and Deming had been master cabinetmakers, but they didn't print their labels with a border that only became popular in the second half of the nineteenth century.

He went into the office. Through the window he saw how the sky had shifted. It was about 2 a.m. None of the files was locked, and he didn't bother with them. There wasn't enough time. Every drawer in the desk was locked. Roman took a ring of thin metal rods from his pants pocket. Working fast, bending a variety of rods of differing lengths, he created a key for each set of tumblers.

He found the typical *gaja* idea of valuables. There were

papers to the house, stocks and bonds, insurance policies, bills of sale, loan notes, memberships in clubs, newspaper clippings with the Sloan name, five hundred dollars in cash, checkbooks, deposit slips and a list of Sloan's customers. There was nothing of recent business that demanded Sloan stay up two nights in a row.

The letters were in the back of the bottom drawer. They were unlike any of the other papers, written in longhand, the address in a girl's rounded manner. There was no return address. There were fifteen in all, and he chose the latest one, postdated a week ago. Roman could hear Hillary now, ". . . who are you to talk about fooling around?"

Dear Hoddinot,

Today passed as slowly as if it were a year. You joke about life being more enjoyable the slower it goes. It's not very funny to me. As it is, I spend all my time thinking about us.

Writing again. The head librarian came by to make sure I was filing. She's jealous because starting Monday, I have a week's vacation and she doesn't want to do the work herself.

Back again. She's finally gone to lunch. At last I can get down to it. I'm sorry it takes so long to work up to things, I'd meant to make it short and sweet. The fact is I meant what I said on the telephone. This is the end. It took a long while to sink in, but now I finally realize that we aren't getting anywhere. Or, I should say, I'm not getting anywhere.

As a matter of fact, I'm just beginning to figure out what a fool I've been. Never being seen with you in public. Sneaking into New York to some sordid hotel and never telling my friends where I'm going and who this fascinating older man is who's going to marry me. Calling you late at night so the servants won't catch on. And why? Because society isn't ready for me yet. I have to be introduced properly to become an eligible wife for Hoddinot Sloan. As if meeting you for weekends in New York was helping me get introduced in Boston! I guess I'm just sick of hearing you say that we just haven't set the date.

This isnt' easy. Ever since you came into the library that day I've been in love with you. Maybe you're in love with me. All I know is that Monday I leave for the Virgin Islands, and when I come back, I have an interview to become a stewardess. I'm good-looking and fairly smart, and they say I shouldn't have any trouble. I know how you feel about stewardesses, but let's admit it, thanks to you I'm no virgin anymore.

So I finally agree with you. I'm too young, too lower-class, too gauche to ever fit into your society. Let's just call it quits and part friends. Don't worry about me; all your secrets are safe.

Love,
Judy

Roman turned to the first page. The letterhead had an embossed script reading: "Judy Mueller." He folded the letter neatly and put it back with the others. Scorpio was searching the middle of the sky as Roman climbed up the trellis to the second floor.

Roman's eyes adjusted to the more complete darkness of his bedroom. There was subtle change in it. The hundred and twenty-five million optical rods that marked man as a night animal reflected faint patterns of light and shadow. The four thin posts of his bed were partially broken, snapped where they rose from the frame and joined over the center of the bed to form a pyramid. Something was moving, though Roman was sure nobody else was in the room.

He turned the flashlight on toward the top of the pyramid. A string hung from it, and the light followed it down to within a foot of the bed, where, slowly describing circles within the open cone, was the frozen ivory grin and matted hair of a devil's head.

12

It was afternoon by the time he got back to New York. Nobody had seen him off at the Sloans'; he'd left before they rose. Because it was Sunday, there were few cars on the streets, and Manhattan's sky was relatively clear. The sidewalks seemed populated entirely by young couples in leather pants and psychedelic shirts walking Afghans and Great Danes. Their parents no doubt had all locked themselves in their apartments with their air conditioners.

When he unlocked the door to his apartment, Dany was there, lying on the sofa, eating unionized grapes, and leafing through fashion magazines. Roman kicked his suitcase under a side chair and threw his jacket and tie over it.

"Hi. I thought you were going to do some shooting on the island this weekend."

"We got it done in one day. The rest of the gang stayed up there, but I decided to come back. In case you did." She held up a center spread hoisery ad. "Don't you think I have better legs?"

"Models are insane."

Dany frowned. He always said that when she asked for his opinion. She had the feeling that he meant it.

He stole a grape from her and ate it. She did have better legs, but he refused to encourage the vanity that served as a soul for a professional model. She was in nothing but an old happy jacket of his, her tan limbs and tilt of the head inviting a phantom photographer with a motorized Nikon to pop up from the other side of the sofa.

"Find what you wanted?" she asked.

"Yeah." He scratched the stubble that was taking over his chin. Even in a tuxedo on the steps of the opera, he'd look as if he had come to hold the place up.

"What was it?"

"A family. The all-American family."

He went to the bathroom to shower off the sweat of the ride and shave. He picked up a roll of adhesive tape and came back into the living room in a towel.

"Jesus Christ," Dany said. A grape stopped an inch from her lips. "What the hell happened to you?"

He raised his arms. "Tape me up, will you?" Last night's activities had irritated the tear. During the shower he'd kept his eyes away from the bruise that ran from his shoulder to his navel. Now that he saw it it hurt.

"A truck run over you?"

"A tree, believe it or not."

She circled him until a wide white band covered part of his chest.

"Looks like a bruised plum," she said, running her finger down the discoloration. "I'm sorry. That wasn't much of a welcome, was it?"

She kissed him, first on the cheek and then on the mouth. Roman's arms found themselves inside the cotton happy jacket. The pain was subsiding.

"Speaking of bruised plums," he said.

"Stop that. You're tickling me."

Hillary's come-on in the field had left its residue of desire. The happy jacket dropped to the floor beside the towel. He pressed Dany into him, conscious as always of the contrast in colors, a contrast that became more marked as contact became more intimate.

"You've gained some weight," he told her. "You'll lose your job, but I like it."

"And what will you do when I lose my job?"

"Get you a crystal ball and teach you how to tell fortunes."

"I'd never be able to tell fortunes. I don't even know what I'm going to be doing a minute from now."

He grinned broadly.

"Well, that, of course," she said.

"Then why fight fate any longer?"

It was four thirty when Roman woke up. The room was in what shade they could get by closing the drapes on an afternoon. Dany, asleep and content, rested her head on his bruised arm. The sheet was down at the foot of the bed so that the air could blow over their bodies. Her breasts sagged slightly to the sides over her rib cage. They were supposed to be a bit too big for her business. What was it that made Americans demand large breasts in their fantasies and flat breasts on their models? To a Romany a woman's breasts were not a sex object. They were out in the open too much, suckling children in a room full of friends or before anyone's eyes on the public road. On Dany, he had to admit, they were sex objects. If she ever succeeded at what she hinted, if they ever did marry, would she suckle her children in front of her friends from Long Island?

Painstakingly he slid his arm out from under her and rolled off the bed. He went into the living room and closed the bedroom door. When he'd put the towel back around his waist, he sat by the telephone with the phone book and opened a fresh pack of cigarettes. He called Pan American first. A recording stalled him for a minute, and then a girl came on the line.

"Hello," Roman said. "This is the First National Bank travel bureau, Mr. Baldwin calling. We would like to check on a reservation made for a Miss Mueller. M-u-e-l-l-e-r. Judy Mueller, for last Monday to the Virgin Islands."

"That would be St. Thomas?" the girl asked.

"That's right. She was supposed to join a tour down there, part of the travel package that we handle. She never did join it. That isn't really that unusual. Often younger clients prefer to disappear on their vacations. But the tour director has just called me to say that her flight is about to leave for the States and Miss Mueller still hasn't shown up. I wonder if you could check your records and tell me whether she made her flight down to the islands."

"Could you tell me the number of her flight?"

"I'm afraid that part of the office is closed on Sundays."

The girl was obviously pondering the request on the other end.

"This is very irregular."

"I understand. But the tour director is very concerned, and so am I. We feel some obligation to our customers to make sure of their well-being."

There was another wait.

"Could I have your name, please, miss?" Roman said. "I'd like to know it the next time I see your supervisor."

"Wait a moment while I ask the computer," she retorted crisply.

Roman was putting out a cigarette when the girl came back.

"We have no Miss Mueller on any flights for St. Thomas last week. What's this all about?"

He hung up.

That was a blank. Pan Am was the only airline he knew of that flew to the Virgin Islands; it was the one Dany had taken the year before. She was tight with her money, though; she would have shopped around. He went back into the bedroom.

"Hey, Dany. Come on. Let's go."

She struggled up on her elbows. "You don't have to lift my eyelid. You know what wakes me up." She rubbed her face. "God."

"I couldn't tell if you were breathing there for a second. You should be glad I checked. Look, when you went to the Virgin Islands with that decorator—"

"He was doing the backgrounds for the bathing suit number. You know that."

"With that decorator, you flew Pan Am. What other airlines go down there?"

"From here?" Dany tried to think through the bleariness of sleep. "Trans Caribbean, but only on Sundays."

"Thanks." He kissed her eyes closed and pushed her

head back down on the pillow. She knew she wouldn't be able to go to sleep again.

He found the number for Trans Caribbean and called. A voice that was a copy of the Pan Am girl's spoke to him. He was disappointed—he'd hoped for some rich, fluty West Indian tones—but he went through his Mr. Baldwin routine enthusiastically. The girl paused at the same points as her Pan Am sister, but she went to check her records, too.

"Hello? Mr. Baldwin? I checked and we did have a reservation for a Miss Mueller. It was paid in advance as you said. But I don't think your tour director should worry. Miss Mueller never boarded the plane; she didn't check in at all. I'm afraid she was a 'Stay Away,' as we call them here."

"Yes." Roman agreed and hung up. He guessed so, too.

"Trouble?" Dany asked. She was at the doorway, picking up the happy jacket with her toes rather than venture in front of the window even though the nearest possible peeping Tom was on the other side of the East River.

"Not exactly. The trouble's gone."

"Antiques?"

"Yeah, antiques."

He had a lost look that came over him very rarely. She crossed the room and pressed his head between her breasts. The maternal gesture revived Roman because it amused him. Maybe she would nurse her kids in public after all.

"I think you should drop the antiques," Dany said, "and get into something interesting."

13

"Bugs?" Captain Frank said. "You're supposed to be getting this murder case out of the way, and you're talking about bugs? I'll tell you about bugs."

He went past Sergeant Isadore to the door and locked it and came back to his desk.

"I'll tell you about bugs," he repeated. "Yesterday I came back here late and what did I find? A CID taping a mike in the men's room, that's what. And a plainclothes going through my wastebasket. That's all. So don't you tell me about bugs."

Isadore pressed his lips together tightly. His round face took on the rigidity of a steel trap shut tight on a small animal. The animal was his tongue.

"Zoologist! He's been too sick to come in? Fine. Keep him away from here. You could have arrested that what's-his-name. Instead you let him get into the warehouse and practically start an antique store. I bet they got a good laugh out of that at CID. Why not give all our suspects a chance to play with the evidence? They can take it out if they like, like a library."

By the time Isadore got a chance to exit, his ears buzzing, he was happy not to hear about bugs either. He turned his anger on Grey. The Gypsy had broken his promise to help. When he got to his desk, he found a note that someone called "Number One Son" had called. If his son showed up, he'd arrest him too.

Isadore stared at the gray Formica top of his desk trying to get hold of himself. Coffee rings merged with cigarette burns which led like exclamations to the crumbs of the Danish he'd had for breakfast. He picked up a crumb on the tip of his finger and ate the evidence. He couldn't arrest his son. As for Grey, he was only acting like a Gypsy. Why had Grey fooled around with the antiques? Was there evidence in the evidence? It was the sort of question that gained baking soda a permanent place in Isadore's heartburn.

An hour later he was at the warehouse of the Astor Movers off Astor Place in the East Village. The friend whose place Buddy Locher had taken the day of the accident was there, having just delivered a van from Boston the day before. The warehouse was nothing more than a pair of truck bays between a used clothes emporium and a hat and felt goods manufacturer. Everything lay under a layer of dust as thick as gray velvet.

Isadore's nerve broke. It was a bad day and a sour case, and a man couldn't be expected to do everything at the same time. He went to a corner newsstand and bought a pack of cigarettes. He lit up on the way to the warehouse. The first drag developed from an innocent experiment to a wicked, lung-stunning inhale. He walked into the empty bay.

"Yeah. What is it?" a man in a dirty mover's uniform asked as he came down a ramp. The uniform stretched over equally beefy arms and stomach.

"I want to—"

"Hey!" the man said. He pointed at Isadore's cigarette and then at a sign posted beside the bay. "Can't you read?"

NO SMOKING IN THE VANS, IN THIS BUILDING OR ON THE JOB, the sign said.

"Everyone's a Surgeon General," Isadore muttered, but he walked out to the street to step on the cigarette. He went back and explained in a deliberately calm fashion who he was and why he came.

"You don't want me," the mover said accusingly. "You want the kid." He went to a metal door, kicked it and yelled, "Hey, Hale. Get down here. Some cop wants to see you." Isadore resisted the impulse to ask whether garbage collecting was good training for moving works of art, but just barely.

"The kid" impressed Isadore more. His name was Howard Washington Hale. He wore his blond hair long but neatly trimmed, and his uniform was crisply white. He was even polite.

"I knew Buddy in the service, but he was a little different," Hale reported. "Not dangerous, just nervous. He didn't send me a letter to say he was coming to Boston, and I bet it was just because he was so relieved to muster out."

"How long have you been out?"

"Six months. I wish I'd been there when Buddy got into town, but there was a party out of town and . . . you know. Don't tell Mr. Astor."

Isadore's jaw dropped. "There is a Mr. Astor?"

"Sure, you just talked to him."

Isadore talked to Hale until the boss reappeared, slamming the door open with one butt of his stomach.

"You still here?" he yelled at Isadore. "I got a schedule to keep. This isn't civil service."

Hale shrugged his shoulders. "Any more questions?"

"No, thanks."

Hale got into the van. Somehow the kid kept it clean even in Astor's warehouse. There was a plastic saint on the dashboard. Isadore remembered it had been among Locher's affects. Astor threatened some cars in the street and waved the van out. Isadore watched it drive to Broadway and wait for the light.

"What is it now?" the mover asked Isadore with anguish.

"Nothing. Thanks, you've been very cooperative, Mr. Astor."

Astor flared. "Okay, okay, so it used to be Astorini. You going to make something out of it? You and the

FBI. You want to see my membership card in the underworld?"

Isadore picked a straight line to his car and tried to follow it. The line was intersected by a bum asking for a cigarette. Isadore handed over his whole pack.

He drove toward the end of Manhattan where the department tow truck dropped vehicles bound as evidence. A pair of young patrolmen were looking over the cars headed for public auction. They passed right over what now looked like a busted accordion but had at one time been an Eldorado. Isadore went to the small van that said LEASED TO ASTOR MOVING on the door. There was no top to the door; it had been sheared off with the top of the cab. He went through the interior for the third time. He didn't expect to find anything he missed at the accident, but Grey's accusations about picking on Gypsies annoyed him. Except for the marks of the collision, the van's cab was spotless, and so was the rear where the antiques were carried. Isadore got out with a sense of absolution and walked to the Eldorado. He'd find a rich field there loaded with possibilities as soon as his expert showed up. His essential optimism was showing through.

Isadore began groaning twenty feet from the Eldorado. He trotted over the damp cement, and by the time he was standing over the crumpled fender he was mentally pounding his breast. No zoologist would help anymore. The Eldorado's body was, for some strange reason, as clean as the van's.

"Yeah," one of the attendants said when Isadore asked. "CID said to hose the place down. Said it was getting to be a health hazard."

It made sense. The Detective Bureau used the lot much more than CID. He and the attendant got the hood open. He looked at the smashed honeycomb of the radiator. The bugs there were washed away, too.

The interior of the car was still dirty, but it had been checked thoroughly. All the contents down to tobacco and pieces of garbage had been sealed in cardboard boxes. The door hung open like a broken wing. The upholstery hardly existed. The lab had taken samples of all stains, and there hadn't been much that wasn't stained in Nanoosh Pulneshti's car. The ashtrays were gone, along with much of the carpet. The dashboard was marked with inscrutable scratches. There was little left of the windshield Nanoosh had gone through. There was nothing left for him to find.

Almost nothing, he admitted. Dirt had collected under the brake pedal, and as a pathetic last note a fungus was growing in it. It reminded him unnecessarily of the humidity of the past few days. In the wreckage of death, life persisted. Isadore was not a callous man.

There was no point going to the driver's side. The door there hadn't opened since the accident. He angled over the floorboard to get a closer look at the fungus. It was a fringe of tiny mushrooms with thin stems and pointed caps. It was a new one on him, and he used to take his boy out mushroom hunting in the Catskills.

"A *pajarito*," Lieutenant Ebert said. He held Isadore's catch into the light with tweezers. The lab technicians had been as stymied as Isadore when he came in with his handkerchief wrapped in a bundle. Ebert was from Narcotics. "How about that? Where in the world did you get it?"

"Then it's not local?"

"I'll say it isn't. You could sell a little treasure like that for five hundred dollars in the East Village. It's from Mexico, the state of Oaxaca just west of Guatemala. The Mazoteca Indians grow some of the best hallucinogenic mushrooms in the world there, *pajaritos*, *derumbes* and big, fat *Santo Jesucristas*. First time I've seen one of these in the city."

The Gypsies hadn't been smuggling the stuff in, Isadore knew, because nothing else like it had been picked up after the accident. These *pajaritos* were just growing, smuggling themselves in.

"What's the germination period for these? I mean, how long would it take them to grow and how fast to die in New York?"

Ebert scratched the bristle that served as hair on his head. Being a "nark" meant he had an active outdoor life and a tan that showed through his crew cut.

"All depends. Fungus's pretty basic stuff. It'll pop up easy enough, but here, in New York, it should die pretty quick. Especially *pajaritos*. I've been down there with the immigration patrol. Cool, damp mountains in the Sierra

Mazoteca. See"—he held his hand out—"these are already dehydrating. So I'd say these could last, once they've started growing, four, five days."

"How long could they have been in the dirt before they started growing."

"Oh, I get you. Considering the change in climate, it would have to be real soon. Less than a week for that, I'd guess, but then nobody knows for sure. Like my friends on the street say, mushrooms are crazy things."

Isadore returned to his desk and sat down with a pencil and pad, feeling a little bit like a girl on the rhythm method. If the *pajaritos*—"little birds," Ebert translated—were about four days old, tops, and the germinating stage was no more than a week, that put the Eldorado in the southern end of Mexico just eleven days ago. This was Friday. The accident had occurred four days before. Which gave Nanoosh Pulneshti less than a week to drive through Mexico and most of the United States. Gypsies were known to be exceptional drivers, but this was pushing it. A week hardly gave Pulneshti enough time to run over a dog, let alone commit, dismember and pack a murder.

He walked around the room. It was mostly empty, just a lieutenant in the corner learning to type. The rest were home having supper. Why wasn't he? On a large corkboard were pictures of kids reported missing by their parents. A file below it held nothing but the names and descriptions of kids who had run away from home or just vanished. Kids who weren't home for supper. He went through the file for the tenth time, picking out those who might bear some resemblance to the body in the bigger file at the morgue. Strict selection winnowed the number down to five.

A high school student from Roanoke, Virginia. A nurse from Brownsville, Texas. Another high school kid from Memphis. A dropout from Little Rock and a social worker from Wheeling, West Virginia. It had to be someone on the road from Mexico, that much he was sure of. If Pulneshti did it. And if Pulneshti didn't do it, he knew less than when he started. The trouble was that Isadore was beginning to suspect that Grey really had learned something.

It took some cajoling, but Erskine Lippincoot of Lippincoot Frères had a weakness for working with the police. When Sergeant Isadore called him on Saturday morning, he took some pleasure in announcing to his weekend guests that he often assisted the authorities in matters dealing with antiques and that they would have to excuse him for a few hours. Duty called, and the Lippincoots had never vacillated in performing civic acts.

Isadore was waiting at the warehouse when Lippincoot arrived in a chauffeur-driven Mercedes. He wadded his gum into a ball and wrapped it in paper as Lippincoot revealed himself in a white twill summer suit and ascot. The two men had never met before, but they recognized each other without difficulty.

"Perhaps you could explain this to me again," Lippincoot said as they entered the warehouse.

"I'll try," Isadore said. "We have some antiques here from an accident. One expert has, uh, already gone over them, but we can't get his report. I'd appreciate it if, with your expertise, you could examine these pieces. Since you are acknowledged to be the top dealer in town and you've been kind enough in the past, we thought you'd help. You see, if you don't find anything, then I'll know that the other man didn't find anything."

"Odd," Lippincoot said, presenting a formidable row of wrinkled brows. "Who is this other man? I'm sure I'd know the name."

"Unfortunately, I can't tell you."

"Very odd."

"It's just to relieve my mind."

Lippincoot's brows met and rebounded. He'd come all the way from Sag Harbor to relieve some sergeant's mind.

"Here they are," Isadore said.

Lippincoot's irritation subsided under the pleasure he always took in fine antiques. Mentally he classified each piece and dismissed the policeman. The tragedy—and masterpiece—of the set, of course, was the highboy, reconstructed so artfully as to almost hide the fact that it was beyond repair.

"Marvelous work, really marvelous. The owner came down to put it back together?" It wasn't the sort of work a police carpenter was capable of.

"No. The other expert. In about an hour," Isadore said. He couldn't help wondering how long it would have taken Erskine Lippincoot.

"Hardly likely." Lippincoot opened a drawer gently. The expressive brows rose further. "That's odd. Why did he do that?"

"What's odd? Did what?"

"The fellow scratched the inside of the drawers, that's all. It's something you might do to authenticate a piece, not put it together. I use a little silver knife for that sort of thing myself."

"On purpose, he did it on purpose?"

"Of course. The man who put this antique together wasn't about to stumble through it. Pine's very soft, and he probably could have managed with any sharp object. I remember, it was during the war, we were in France, and I had nothing but a nail file. . . ."

"Pull them out. All the drawers."

"On, no," Lippincoot protested. "This is dried walnut that's two hundred years old. Very brittle and just held together with epoxy. It could fall apart if we began man-handling it."

"Pull them out," Isadore ordered in the tone of voice he used on rookies. Somewhere in that circumference of fat was a steel core, Lippincoot realized, and he obediently pulled the drawers out one by one and laid them on the floor.

"Odd."

Understatement was starting to wear on Isadore, but he inquired politely what provoked the remark.

"You cut to see if wormholes are genuine," Lippincoot informed him. "These are. They're regular capillaries wormholes, and that's where you run into some of your troubles with refinishing. Sucks moisture in, thus. And there's a definite residue in some of these. Recent I'd even say, though it's hardly noticeable."

"Residue of what?"

"Oh, blood, of course. I am an expert, you know."

Lippincoot was unwavering in his opinion. Asked whether there was any evidence in the drawers of dry ice, the dealer said just the warping in the joins.

"An insurance agent checked it?" he wanted to know.

"That doesn't mean anything if the man's late for lunch or something. You don't look for smuggling in a Chippendale chest, you know, just to see if someone had knocked a hole in the side. You can't place too much in what insurance agents say, you see. As a group, they're very. . . ."

"Odd," Isadore supplied.

There were a round dozen girls missing from the New England area, Isadore discovered when he got back to the office. Half of them were suspected of skipping off to cut cane in Cuba. Four others for color of hair, build or easily identified marks were disqualified. That left a private school teacher from Middlebury, Connecticut, and a librarian from Boston. There were no fingerprints on either that he could match with the corpse. It took an extra day, but he had Middlebury and Boston get hold of the girls' dentists and check out the dental profile. By Sunday afternoon he knew the corpse to be one Judith Jean Mueller.

14

A submarine bobbed in the brackish water. Its batteries had run down, and its crew propellers were still. Radio signals failed. Its skipper, a twelve-year-old boy, looked at it in frustration. He turned the knobs on his transmitter back and forth. With technology a failure, he went off into the park to find a long stick.

"I suppose you've told all Nanoosh's relatives, the ones you couldn't find before. They're pleased," Isadore said, gesturing with a hot dog.

"If I could find them, I'd tell them, and they'd probably be ecstatic. Thanks to you."

"Tell them they're welcome."

The two men were sitting on a bench beside the boat pond. Behind them rose a treelined edge of Central Park and above that the luxury apartments of the East Side in a skyline like a dingy graph.

"It makes more sense. One thing always did bother me," Isadore said, licking a dab of mustard from a finger. "Why in the world would a Gypsy who was racing across the country stop off to commit a murder?"

"People have told me it's possible."

Isadore winced. "You know what I mean. Now Sloan makes sense. There's a reasonable combination of motive and opportunity there. In fact, a lovely one."

"Boy gets girl, boy loses girl, boy kills girl."

"Uh-huh." Isadore wasn't sure whether he was being teased or not. He turned with Roman to look at the boy, who was batting the water with a branch that was too short. "The Mueller girl was reported missing by her roommate. The roommate knew everything about Miss Mueller's romance with Sloan except his name. He was some wealthy, older society guy who seduced her and then went back on his proposal. The marriage proposal, that is. The roommate never saw him, just his car when he parked outside and honked. It was a lemon Buick station wagon. She never got the license plate, but she remembered that she saw a scrape on the right rear fender when the Mueller girl left that last night.

"It didn't take long to find the car. The scrape came from an accident reported a week before when Sloan's daughter was driving it. As soon as the Boston police took the roommate around to Sloan's place, she saw the car. It was the same one.

"And then everything cracked. The roommate told us Mueller and her boyfriend went off for weekends in New York. We didn't get anything from the desk clerks, but Sloan was so cheap he used his credit card. That gave us enough to tackle Sloan last night. He denied everything, naturally, until we found the letters in the desk. Then he said it was all a mistake. They were close, but the girl was exaggerating: He made no promises about getting married, and of course, he never killed her."

The submarine had submerged. The boy was throwing rocks in the water from frustration. The two men moved farther down the bench to avoid getting wet. Isadore wiped his hands with his paper napkin, folded the paper neatly, and put it in his pocket.

"Did he?" Roman asked innocently.

"It's pretty plain that he did. Nice girl, good reputation, a little bookish, ripe for some character like Sloan. Sooner or later she finds out that she's been had, and in a last scene she threatens to let the affair out. If she's not good enough for the society page, she'll make sure he isn't either. A man like Sloan, it's the most important thing in the world. He kills her in a rage, cuts her up in his little workshop and stuffs her in the chest of drawers."

"Highboy."

"Highboy, lowboy, who cares? Packs her off to the Armory Show in New York in a panic. He figures he can always pull the chest out of his exhibit once it's at the Armory and dispose of the body. The main thing is to get it out of Massachusetts. Maybe he'll toss it in the Hudson; he doesn't know, he's no professional. Then he hits the jackpot. The insurance company calls him up and says there's been an accident, his pieces have been badly damaged. By the way, they say, he might be interested in knowing that the accident caught a desperate murderer who was carrying a mutilated body around. The murderer died in the accident.

"Talk about luck. He was wondering what the hell he was going to do with that body, and the body takes care of itself. What's better, he's not sending anyone else to jail because they're dead already. God is smiling on Hoddinot Sloan. All he has to do is lay low and take the insurance money. He might even make a profit. Isn't that what Calvinism is all about?"

"You're a learned man, Mr. Isadore."

"I know what makes sense, that's all, and this makes sense. Murders always do in some crazy way. And murderers are such cocky bastards. The Boston police told me Sloan practically fainted when they told him the roommate decided she'd seen him pick the Mueller girl up that last night when she disappeared," Isadore said.

"He denied it?"

"No. By that time he was screaming for his lawyer. And when his lawyer got there and Sloan discovered he could only handle codicils, he screamed for another one. I'm taking the train up this afternoon. If I'm lucky, I'll get to be the one who tells him about the blood on the saw. It's the Mueller girl's type. I just wanted to let you know what happened before I went because I gave you sort of a rough time. It's okay?"

"Sure," Roman said. Isadore really did care whether they were still friends.

"Besides, you gave us a lead with that chest, you know.

Made me look at it a second time. How come you didn't tell me about it?"

Roman shrugged. "I found it; but I didn't know what to do about it, and I didn't even know what I'd found. I'm no detective like you." He paused. "Sloan's the man, huh?"

Isadore tried to read something in the Gypsy's black eyes and gave up. "Right. Anyway, I'm happy about the way things worked out. Don't tell me you're not?"

Roman laughed. "It's in your hands now, Sergeant."

"Hey, I've got to go. My train leaves in an hour, and Number One Son is driving me to the station. I've got to give him plenty of time."

Roman watched Isadore's slouched figure move away down the border of the pond and up the stairs that led to Seventy-second Street. In the water, the boy was wading toward his ship with hands out as if he were walking on a tightrope.

Roman walked away from the park toward his apartment to get ready for a party. Vera's *kumpania* would not only be celebrating the clearing of Nanoosh's name but also the marriage of her daughter Laza to a boy from a *kumpania* in Queens.

Dany was in a pout when he got home. She had been insinuating herself more and more into his life, waking him in the morning with a phone call, rushing off to a model's call, visiting his shop at lunch, rushing off for another shooting, coming back to cook supper and make love. If she wasn't any closer to getting married, she was making him feel very guilty.

"I don't think they'd be so upset because of one *gaji*," she said. "How am I ever going to meet your friends, anyway? I mean, I know some of the men, but I've never met any of the women."

Roman painted his face with lather. It was impossible trying to tell her that he was separating her from the Gypsy women for her own good. A *gaji* who married a Rom was treated as a slave by every Gypsy woman. She would have to fulfill every Gypsy duty and custom, from changing from Givenchy's to crude petticoats to learning the exacting, sometimes humiliating business of *duikkerin* fortunes. Not that he needed the money, but the women would demand it. He and Dany were better off as they were. He only wished he could find something to change the subject. As he started to shave, a thin red line appeared along his scar.

"Damn it, Dany, you shaved your legs with my razor again. I gave you your own."

"It was dull."

"Then change it." He slipped a fresh blade into his razor. She was hovering right outside the bathroom door; he could sense it. Usually, he had no trouble handling her moods, turning her anger into a joke they could both laugh at. There were times, though, when he seemed to be paralyzed, and her obvious, even childish manipulations would drive him mad. "It's not just a party," he told her between strokes. "No strangers are allowed at weddings. Not even priests. Another time would be better. You want to like them, right?"

He looked up and saw her in the mirror. She was biting her false fingernails, a bad sign. He hid by ducking into the sink basin and washing off the lather. When he was dry, he slipped a fresh shirt on and went into the living room. On the table were the bottle of anisette and felt bag weighted with gold eagles for Laza's new *gonya* he would take with him.

"So, you are going to the party and just leaving me here," Dany crowed triumphantly. She sat with her arms crossed beside the door.

"Come on, Dany, be fair. I called you and told you about this, and you said it was fine because some speechwriter had asked you out."

"The one who said he wanted to improve my mind?" she snorted.

"That's right, the one who wanted to improve your mind."

"Very funny," she said with the recurring air of triumph.

He let his arms sag, unequally because one of them held the heavy bag. The only *gaji* in the world that had the power to confuse him was this obstinate, intriguing, practically unread (not including *Vogue*), soap-operatic, almost skinny, silky, passionate, damp-eyed model.

"There are a hundred parties in town that you could go to tonight if you wanted to," he said.

"I'll stay here if you don't mind. I think I'll read in bed." She saw that that was going down pretty hard, so she added, "And maybe there's something on television."

"Whatever you want."

When he left and while he was waiting for the elevator, Dany opened the door again and slammed it.

Why was he feeling like Hoddinot Sloan?

15

Vera was happy because Laza would not have been able to marry for some time if Nanoosh's name had not been cleared. Roman explained to her on the phone that Sergeant Isadore solved the crime, but as far as she and her *kumpania* were concerned, they had asked Roman to save Nanoosh's *mulo* from limbo, and in a week that was what happened. Their low opinion of the police accepted no other interpretation. Now they could celebrate.

All the curtains inside the *ofisa* were pulled aside so that the party covered the entire floor from the back to the front of the building. Folding tables were placed together and decorated with colorful cloths. On them were plates of cold cuts, barbecued chickens, meat-stuffed pancakes called *bokoli*, pink beef with a sharp scent of rosemary, pork roast with liquorice aniseed, a holiday goose redolent of sage and marjoram, more chickens, and from somewhere an enormous glistening suckling pig. Surrounding these, as if the point of honor was to leave no inch of the table bare, were smaller bowls of yogurt with sesame or lettuce or cucumbers or tomatoes. Women shoved these together to make room for slippery white beans in vinegar, chick-peas in sesame paste and green beans in sour cream. The men spiced their thirsts with lentils and cheese and small, salty ripe olives. Children reached for honeyed pastries, meat balls rolled in nutmeg and chilly squares of eggplant that ringed fragile mountains of fresh black bread. At one end of the long line of tables a brother of the groom pumped beer from the kegs around him like a happy madman trying to explode a cache of dynamite lost in the profusion.

"It is a very good match," Vera announced into Roman's ear. "Dodo came to me the other day about his boy as if he had a present. Him with those two apes of brothers with the chicken in their hands." She pointed with a hunk of pork. "They offered only five hundred dollars if you can believe it."

Roman shook his head with simulated wonder. What did make him wonder was how Vera was able to speak above the din of spontaneous singing, dancing, bragging and two competing record players, one with the rhapsodies of Balogh Istvan and the other with the flamencos of Manitas de Plata.

"Romano, I ask you. Five hundred dollars for a sweet girl like Laza! Sweet-tempered, hardworking, beautiful like a plum, knows how to *duiker* like a grandmother, can go into J.C. Penney's and come out with an electric stove nobody sees her. For a boy like Kalia. Dumb, bad-mannered, ugly. I pity his mother. All he thinks about is cars, and he gets caught stealing those. As a favor, just so as not to dishonor Dodo in front of his own brothers, I ask four thousand dollars. It's the least I can do for Laza."

One of his friends gave Roman a fresh beer and tried to take him away by the arm, but Vera hung on.

"So we sat down and discussed it," she shouted. "Perhaps Kalia wasn't such a bad boy after all. Remember how he made that car out of nothing but stolen parts, and for just being sixteen he seems to be pretty lucky at the racetrack. Laza, even I'll admit, has a taste for expensive things, and sometimes she has to pay for them. I mean, it wasn't all black and white. Dodo offered a thousand, and I came down a little to thirty-five hundred for courtesy."

"For courtesy."

"Yes. Then it was mentioned that Dodo's *kumpania* was

one of the oldest and most respected in the country and had really a very good lawyer that they would lend us since we would be related and offered fifteen hundred. Someone also mentioned Laza couldn't cook old shoes, which I denied, but Dodo and his family have been guests of mine before and I came down to two thousand seven hundred and fifty."

"Very wise," Roman said. It was easier to talk now since they were being crushed together by people clearing a circle for dancing.

"Then, naturally, there was the human aspect," Vera said with a tragic, tolerant sigh that shamed the fact that her feet were barely touching the floor from the squeeze. "It seems that Laza and Kalia do feel some affection for each other and wanted to marry. So, for twenty-five hundred dollars, I gave in."

All of Vera's *kumpania* of more than forty Romanies and Dodo's *kumpania* of fifty and a hundred or more guests were jostling in as many different directions in the crowded *ofisa*. Men who had not seen each other for days and others who had just come back from years of wandering through Europe were seizing old friends and inventing toasts. Their wives were just as forceably shaping huddled atolls of gossip. The *shavs*, small boys and girls, wended their way through legs to the tables to fill themselves with sweet pastries. A large hand came through the mass and snatched Roman away from Vera like a card in a magician's hand.

"Romano! Romano! So this is our detective!"

Kore Tshatshimo, a giant with ringlets hanging over a genially misshapen face, slapped Roman on both shoulders and then smothered him in an embrace that took his breath away. Roman squeezed him back until he could feel Kore's ribs shifting. Kore howled with pleasure.

"The same," he said. "All this talk about you going soft. I said that the day Romano Gry becomes a *gajo* is the day I put on a skirt. Ha, remember that time we were in Rio and the soldiers tried to make us show identification cards. Ah? Yes?"

"I can't forget." How could he? That was the time Kore kicked a patrol car into the Atlantic.

"And you and Nanoosh took their uniforms and put

them on and went and arrested those girls," Kore said before remembering that Nanoosh was dead. To cover any
sacrilege, he offered a toast. "To Nanoosh."

They drank, and Kore brightened up.

"You know, it's a good thing you got that killer. Laza's
been trying to run away with Kalia for the last month, I
hear. Vera couldn't get her married off soon enough.
Besides, I think it's a good thing, a marriage now. Everyone has been very unhappy about Nanoosh. This will take
their minds off it."

"A toast to happiness," Roman said, knowing a cue
when he heard it. A procession of mugs passed through his
hands along with the toasts. Since he was a hero, everyone
wanted a drink with him, and Kore wanted to match everyone's toast. All the men had contributed liquor, so a
blend of cognac, carbonated wine, anisette, vodka, brandy
and beer rolled through his stomach and up to his head.
On a table that had been stripped of its food, the guests
were depositing their gifts in columns of gold coins and
disheveled wads of paper money, the start of Laza and
Kalia's *sumadjii*, a portable heirloom and treasure.

Dodo and Kore sat Roman on a chair for a *patshiv* to
be sung in his honor by one of Kalia's brothers. He was a
lean boy with a Spanish guitar. A grizzled old man stood
behind him with a violin, waiting for the boy to begin.
The boy waited with his eyes closed until the crowd in the
ofisa had become silent, and then he sang.

It started as a high, emotional keening, the boy's head
thrown back in sorrow as he told of the shock of
Nanoosh's death. The Romani tongue, a dark Indian
opalescent stone lacquered with singing for the Persians,
slaving for the Magyars, and dying in every corner of the
earth, filled the room and their hearts. Guttural but light
as a bird swooping through the night, traditional and un-
predictable, something that delighted in melody and then
ignored it for a stronger impulse made the ring of men
and women and the children sitting on the floor all hold
their breath. This was their story, their history coming
from the young boy and the old man, and when the *pat-
shivaki djili* came to its exploding, victorious close with
the identification of the murderous *gajo*, two hundred
people were clapping and crying.

One song was not enough. It was the old man's turn with a *djili* centuries older than himself that came out in practically a whisper. With a show of extreme reluctance, an elder with a white mustache that came down to his collar allowed himself to be pushed into the middle of the circle. His hands lifted over his head, he began to dance, at first awkwardly, and then, as the spirit coursed through him like new blood, with a recall of vigor and grace that drew shouts of appreciation from his grandchildren. When he tired, another ancient took his place. When all the elders had danced, the *shavs* took over, slapping their hands together and shouting, inspired by the admiration of the girls who watched.

"All this is really for you, Romano," Kore said with great solemnity but a little unsteadily. By now even his bulk had been saturated with alcohol. "Imagine, trying to say a Lovara would kill a girl. That is a *gaja* vice. A Rom might hit a woman, but kill her? Never! Unless, of course, he was Gitano." Kore, like most Kalderash and Lovari, had a great distrust for the Spanish Gypsies.

The music stopped, and into the middle of the circle stepped Vera and Dodo. Kalia's father held a bottle of Courvoisier. Around the neck of the bottle was a string of gold pieces which marked the brandy as the *pliashka*. The bottle was opened and poured into two glasses from which Dodo and Vera drank soberly. When they embraced, their children were married. Later there would be a ceremony by a sympathetic priest, but it would be only for form. The Romany signified their recognition of the union now with cheers from the women and drinks for the men.

So far Kalia and Laza had been invisible. The groom had been driving up and down Broadway with some of his closest friends while the bride stayed at another *ofisa* with a friend and an aunt. At this point she was brought to Vera's and escorted to the kitchen to wait for Kalia. It was a necessary part of the tradition that she be carried off struggling by her husband.

The drinking and talking and singing carried on for another hour until Kalia arrived. The signal was passed back to the kitchen, where Vera hurriedly unbraided Laza's long hair. The girl stared down at the white silk dress bought specially for the occasion. With a tenderness that surprised Laza, Vera sang very softly:

> *Kay hin m'ro vodyi?*
> *Ujes hin cavo,*
> *Ujes sar o kam,*
> *Ujes sar pani,*
> *Ujes sar kumut,*
> *Ujes sar legujes,*
> *Pen mange,*
> *Caveskro vasteha*
> *Kay hin m'ro vodyi?*

In another language it would mean, "Where is my heart? The child is pure, pure as the sun, pure as the water, pure as the moon, pure as the purest. So tell me, how could the child steal my heart?"

There was a knock on the kitchen door, and the girl went out alone. In a line waiting for her were her brothers and cousins forming a shield. Coming across the room toward them were Kalia and his brothers and cousins. The two small armies met and engaged in a spectacular Hollywood stuntman sort of battle that Kalia's side was ordained by custom to win. He grabbed Laza around the waist and started to drag her away. She screamed and pushed him away violently, but he refused to let go. They fell to the floor once, and when he still pulled her to the door. Laza tore at her hair with fear and scratched her face while the spectators moved out of the way of the shrill elopement. The bride made one last desperate effort to break loose, and then Kalia had forced her through the door and was dragging her down the steps to her accompaniment. At last, he threw her in the car and drove off.

Kore took a cigarette from Roman, lit it and let out a judicious blue plume of smoke. "Very good. She did her family honor. It's not often you see nice kids like that, Romano."

Roman wondered whether a marriage like this would appeal to Dany's hysterical instincts. Kore had picked up a keg on each shoulder and danced while Roman accompanied him with claps. Dodo and his brothers joined in with a song. Vera laughed at one side, her necklace of coins slapping against her bosom. Dodo's brothers forced toasts of beer and Tokay onto Roman. As he danced, Kore's amulet, a seashell inscribed with stars, fell out of his shirt and danced on a chain. For a passing moment it became a devil's head.

Roman wasn't drunk. He was thinking more clearly than he had all day. Something in the back of his mind was eating the brandy and beer like a demon. It was evil. Its outline was large and ominous. "There are no hesitation wounds," he remembered. It was capable of bending the posts of a bed, let alone dance with kegs on its shoulders. It had killed the girl and Nanoosh, and it could have killed him too if it had wanted to. It was not an outline of Hoddinot Sloan.

For the first time he admitted to himself what he shared with Sloan. The dry, pretentious, unpleasant *gajo* was also in love. Why else would he save the letters and wait up for hours for a phone call from a girl he had murdered?

16

Celie Miyeyeshti was an important woman by a number of definitions. To begin with she was a mountain of a woman whose petticoats made pleated foothills. When she sat, her great-grandchildren raced to put at least two folding chairs side by side. Among Romanies, the word "important" was the most common polite description of someone with weight, and Celie Miyeyeshti was the most important woman in New York.

Besides that, she was a *phuri dai*, a woman acknowledged to have such extraordinary powers of perception and such understanding of the unwritten laws of Romany that children and formidable members of the *Kris* alike would modestly bring their problems to the garish, mammoth crone on her folding throne. No one knew how old she was. Her passports gave a variety of guesses, just as they differed on her nationality. She traveled in the rear of her Fleetwood Cadillac limousine with jump seats for anyone who cared to stuff themselves into the vast car with her as she dispensed wisdom—where to rent an *ofisa*, when to attempt a *bozur*, what crime was great enough to assemble the *Kris*—with an air of mystery that was almost sexual. Early in the morning, when Laza and Kalia had consummated their wedding and the bloodstained proof of virginity had been displayed, Celie would face the weary couple. She would break a loaf of bread and put a pinch of salt on each piece and offer them to Laza and Kalia, saying, "When you are tired of this bread and this salt, then you will be tired of one another." Laza and Kalia would exchange their halves and eat them as the children threw handfuls of rice over their heads, and yet another round of celebration would begin.

"Get this Romano a chair," Celie ordered. A tiny girl slid a chair behind Roman.

"Thank you," Roman said. He wiped the sweat off his forehead and looked at Celie. Somehow she remained cool in the Spanish mantilla and virtual breastplate of necklaces of strung coins she always wore to parties. Gold seemed to permeate her; it winked from twenty teeth when she smiled.

"You should learn to relax," Celie said. "If everything is over, why aren't you relaxing? What did you want to ask me?"

He wondered what it was that gave him away. No matter, he was good at reading people but she saw things that he wouldn't in a thousand years. She knew that for once he wasn't sitting next to her to banter about her girth.

"I don't know," he said.

Over by the tables, Kore and Dodo were pretending to be an Oursari and his bear. The boy who had sung the *patshiv djili* was singing an emotional *canto hondo* he'd learned in Granada. Two women were arguing over who had made the better *bokoli*. Children attacked each other with bread clubs. When one threw a disputed *bokoli*, the din became worse. A circle of elders began singing the old songs, and in a few minutes when their second wind came back, they would start dancing, too.

"Come," Celie said as she heaved herself out of her chairs, "this is no place to talk about death."

Roman followed her as she plowed her way with dignity back through the *ofisa* to the empty kitchen.

Dany finished chewing one side of her lower lip and started on the other. Her oversized glasses rested on the end of her nose, the lenses glazed by the blue of the television screen. Without them, anything beyond ten feet was a blur. Contact lenses made her eyes tear, which created new problems. She wouldn't wear anything but contacts in public, and Roman did nothing but make fun of her as she alternated, while they strolled in front of Harry Winston's, between lighthearted smiles and Kleenex.

That was another reason to hate him, to add to all the others she'd thought of during the evening. On the television, an enormous iguana was terrorizing Japan. It was a boring, stupid movie, and it scared her, and that was another reason for hating him for leaving her alone.

She shifted on the sofa, pulling a pillow over her stomach. It was a warm night, so she was in nothing but his old kimono, and since she'd turned all the air conditioners on full blast, she was freezing. She glanced at her watch. It was two thirty, and she had enough precious gems of enmity to stock her for a month.

Roman had promised that he'd come back early, and she was amazed at her own acuity of hearing each time the elevator moved. Dany knew what she was going to say. She wasn't going to say a thing, just let him stew in guilt. Later, in the morning, she would let him make up. As the hundred-foot iguana ate a tank in the middle of downtown Tokyo, she held the pillow tighter.

The elevator stopped on her floor. It had to be Roman because the apartment was on the top floor and his neighbor was in Europe. It was too late to turn the set off, so she grabbed the book on the floor and began reading the last pages of Spinoza. There was no key in the door, and she was putting the book back down when the bell rang. She jumped and laughed at herself. He'd know that she was up waiting for him.

Dany took her time, checking herself in the mirror, tying the sash tight and assuming a look of displeasure. She took the chain off the door and opened it. Before she could close it again, the heel of a hand shot through, staggering her. She tried to keep her balance, holding onto the antenna of the television, when the hand came down a second time over her mouth. As she tried to pull free, another hand gripped the back of her neck. The antenna snapped off as she was dragged back onto the sofa.

There were five of them, all dressed brightly in thick pullover ski masks, windbreakers and ski gloves. The heat of the night was already making them sweat in their costumes, so their eyelids batted.

"The lock, the lock," the one holding her whispered.

The chain was shot, and they turned back to her. Dany reached back to scratch, and her hands were grabbed and twisted down behind her back. Something bit into her wrists as they were tied together, and she was thrown onto her face. She was smothering in the pillow, and at last her head was wrenched back by the hair, and she inhaled once before a balled-up nylon stocking was pushed into her mouth. One of Roman's socks was tied over her eyes.

It was ridiculous, she knew, but what she thought of was that the kimono was pushed up on her back during the struggle and her rear was uncovered. She knew that she should fight some more no matter how futile it was, but that would expose her completely. She squeezed her legs together and concentrated on not throwing up on the gag. On the floor, she could hear the crack of her glasses being crushed by a heel.

"Take it easy," the whisperer said into her ear, his hand resting familiarly on a bare buttock. "Just take it easy and nod. Now, is he coming back?"

Dany shook her head. She was crying and cursing herself for being so weak. The worst they could do was rape her, she told herself. Then a hand closed on her nostrils, clamping the cartilage hard, and her blinded eyes shot open as she realized what they could do. The grip on her nose loosened, and she sucked in air.

"I'll ask you again. Is he coming back tonight?"

As soon as she started to shake her head again, the hand regained its grip. She couldn't escape it. A fingernail dug through the skin. In a black vacuum, she saw with utter clarity that she was being killed. She'd swallowed the nylon gag back into her throat. When she tried to roll off the sofa, two more hands held her ankles. It took her forever to understand that the brittle snap was the cartilage bending in that inescapable grip. That the twin pops were the feeble protests of her eardrums. The sofa seemed to open up, like a cushioned coffin.

Death was a stream. An iguana changed colors as it

gained on her. It grasped her toes and climbed up to rest on her soft instep. Floating, she couldn't shake it off. When it had regained its breath, the lizard started climbing up over her ankle, to her calf, tickling her as it dragged itself over the back of her knee. Its sharp feet dug into the meat of her thighs as it continued its journey. When it raised itself over the shuddering flesh of her buttocks, its footsteps became strangely louder, crashing, deafening. Then she felt the cool touch of its split tongue on the base of her spine and she could stand it no longer. She escaped from her body.

"Hey, she's having convulsions and throwing up."

"Make the gag tighter."

She couldn't escape. Somewhere in her mouth and nose, clots of her were caught. The crashes became louder, more distinct.

"She's choking on the stuff."

"I can't stand it. Cover her somebody, please."

"She'll survive."

The footsteps were inside her, running with dull, heavy thuds, racing and shaking her with each step. Then, with amazement, she recognized her heart. And the acrid taste of vomit in her mouth, and the fact that she wasn't dead. Something warm touched her.

"I'm sorry, I had to cover her," a girl said.

"Whisper, God damn it, whisper. She can hear you," said the voice that she identified best. "Turn up the TV."

It was wonderful to hear the shrieks of the horror movie again. She couldn't have been under for more than a few minutes. Her ears hurt but unusual sounds, besides the screaming of film extras, came through. The noise of a drawer being opened and the disjointed clatter of its contents on the floor. A curtain being carefully, maliciously ripped apart. An antique chair caromed off the wall by insane force.

When was he coming back, they'd asked. He was already late. He was probably rushing home now, she thought. They were tearing the place apart because they didn't have their hands on him. She began praying that he was drunk, that his friends were holding onto him, keeping him, that he was flirting with a girl, anything. The chill sound of glass being scratched filled the room. Nobody else would hear it. The people downstairs were away on vacation too.

"It's your fault. You said he was home."

"The lights were on," a male voice answered.

"Don't throw the china. Use a hammer."

They knew she was awake because they all were whispering again. It was difficult to tell which was a man and which a woman.

"It's Sèvres."

"Give me that hammer."

The china cup exploded like a gunshot. As the unseen phantoms went on with their destruction, the rest of the fragile set went off like a child's string of firecrackers. She huddled in the blanket, shivering, her tongue pulled away from the stocking, hoping that they were done with her.

"There's a safe behind the bed. Let's open it."

She heard them pull the bed back, and then there was a relative silence as they attempted to find the correct combination. Failure was marked with the report of a hammer and the renewed zeal with which they attacked the rest of the apartment. She was getting better at images now. She could picture the knife that penetrated the cushion of a chair and ripped out the stuffing in manic jerks.

How long had they been here, she wondered. Her fright gathered when she realized that there must be almost nothing left to destroy in the apartment. Every chair or table or mirror or piece of china, everything had been smashed but her. They would be left standing with their hammers and knives and hands with only one target left. The strange cacophony had longer and longer pauses. Before, she'd wanted it to end. Now she was willing for it to go on forever.

The room was silent, except for the panting of people who had been working very hard on a summer's night in woolen masks. Somehow she knew the colorful masks and gloves were still on. How nice it would be to go skiing with Roman in New England, in the White Mountains. She'd never done that.

The sofa sagged. Someone was sitting next to her. She felt the heat on the side of her face when he bent to speak to her.

"We have to go. We're going right now," the whisperer

said in a pleasant, conversational tone. The hope leaped in her even while she tried to fight it. She made her body as absolutely still as possible. A hand ran along her ribs.

"We have to go," he repeated. "But we can't just go. Do you know what I mean. We can't just go."

The hope died stillborn.

"Give me the razor," he said: and she knew he wasn't talking to her anymore. It was stupid, of course, because the sock was around her eyes but she closed her eyes anyway so that she wouldn't see what he was doing because she was a stupid girl, as Roman always said, and that was the way she'd die.

At least she knew enough to pass out when he started.

Celie balanced the glass of hot tea between the fingertips of her hands so that it looked like an offering to a bizarre buddha. She blew a wisp of steam away and gave the glass to Roman.

"You're a smart boy. Romano. I always said that. You may be right, and I may be right, since we're both so smart. But let me tell you something wise. Stay out of it. It's *gaja* business, not yours."

"You said that before."

"Because I know when you're not listening to me. Nanoosh is safe. That's all that concerns you."

"He threatened me with the devil's head."

"Bah. That doesn't frighten you, and I know it. It shows how much he really knows about the rites."

"It shows that he thinks he knows. That's what makes him dangerous." He thought back on Sloan, the coward who paced for hours in his office waiting for his phone call, who went to bed to have bad dreams. The man who left the devil's head had come in through the bedroom window the same as Roman. Roman would have heard him if he had entered the house by a door. It was a man who was as at home in the dark as Roman. "The only reason he didn't kill me was that I was at the house. It would have been too coincidental for the police. He knows what I am."

"You think that this evil thing is after you in particular? I have news for you, *gaja* evil is more impersonal than that. You can step aside and let it go on its way, and it will forget all about Romano Gry."

"And what do you suggest I do tomorrow night? Not think about it?"

The sound of the party wasn't enough to overcome the silence in the kitchen. A pin from Laza's dress was on the floor, and Roman pushed it aside with his foot.

"All right," Celie said finally. "You are such a *phral* of this policeman, why don't you tell him?"

It was quite a concession for Celie to make. No Rom spoke to the police. Only her dispensation would allow Roman to in the eyes of the *kumpanias*.

"No good," he said. "Isadore has a suspect, I have someone I've never seen, a phantom. He has his evidence and motive. All I can say is that there will be another murder. Do you think that courts admit Gypsies with stories about devils and dark ceremonies? I've seen the murder weapon, and so have you. Isadore wouldn't know what I was talking about. Besides, Isadore could take the killer to a ball game and not know it. If I saw him, I would know him in an instant."

"Then let the *gaja* fight their own battles," Celie said. "If they don't know how to, that's their problem. Phew, now you've ruined my evening."

He'd never seen Celie angry before, and shrugging his shoulders didn't help.

"Let me tell you another secret since you're so interested in them," she said. "We are in America, right?"

"Right."

"You even go around with an American girl, don't you?"

"Uh-huh."

"Do you consider yourself an American? Because if you do, I consider you a great fool. How long has this America been around, two hundred years? Well, the Romanies have been around for five thousand years, longer than any nation. And why? Because we know how to survive. The Aryans tried to kill us, the Persians, the Tartars, the Magyars, the Africans, the Germans, everybody. But we stay together, and we move on, and we keep one thing in mind, to survive, and that is our greatest secret. As soon as you stop thinking of yourself as a Rom and as something else then, Romano, you are already a dead man. And when they come to my door to tell me about your brave death, I will say *bater*, so be it."

Roman looked down at the pin. He forgot whether it was good luck or bad to pick it up. It was after three, and he'd promised to be back long ago, and he was tired. Celie had been battering him for an hour.

"I wouldn't have told you what you wanted to know if I'd suspected what you wanted to do," she said. "You are a favorite, so you were able to hide it from me. It wasn't fair. So I am not going to let you go until you promise that this is the end. Because you have involved me, I can demand this. You will do nothing. You will let the *gaja* murder themselves and catch themselves. I forbid you to have anything more to do with it."

The ageless black eyes looked into his.

"Do you promise?"

He sighed and put the glass on a counter. The side of the glass was smeared with jam. A tart aroma rose from it, a heady aroma he'd smelled a thousand different times and places before.

"Yes," he answered.

Kore had a new song he wanted Roman to hear when he walked out of the kitchen. Yojo was opening a fresh bottle of brandy. Roman begged off and was about to leave when the newlyweds returned. Laza glowed in response to the awed giggles of her former playmates. Vera spread her arms wide to reveal a bedsheet spangled with bloodstains.

Roman didn't get home until after four, and then he found his promise already broken.

17

The apartment looked as if it had been picked up and shaken in the teeth of a monster. Slashed paintings and broken mirrors lay on the floor amid china shards. Chairs had been denuded of their legs and splats. A torn curtain dragged on the floor, stirring a little from the air wandering in from the broken window. In the haphazard destruction, it took Roman a moment to pick out her arm.

A memory emerged of a childhood enemy who had one winter unexpectedly pushed him into a deep creek—the same frozen, heavy, helpless shock. He pulled the blanket off her, moving quickly as an antidote to fear, untying the blindfold of his own sock and the scarf around her wrists. Her hands were cold, and one arm was daubed with blood. Something was hanging from the corner of her mouth, and he watched with horror as a whole nylon stocking came out when he pulled.

It was impossible to tell whether she was breathing and he put his hand between her breasts, and the frozen sensation thawed into sweat when he felt her heart beating shallowly in sleep. The vandals had left a decanter of brandy in the kitchen untouched. Roman lifted Dany's head to pour a glass into her mouth. She choked, and he sat her up, holding her upright against his shoulder. The nearer she dared come to consciousness, the closer he held her until finally they were rocking together on the sofa in the middle of the shattered room with the night air coming through the paneless windows.

"What a dump," Dany said in an imitation of Liz Taylor doing an imitation of Bette Davis. It was an hour later, and she was coming around. They were sitting on the bed, the scene of least damage. The bathroom medicine cabinet had been emptied into the tub, and the contents of the refrigerator had been emptied everywhere. She was eating a reasonably clean breakfast roll for her empty stomach.

"How's the arm feel?"

"Fine, I don't even notice it. It'll heal in a couple of days. As a matter of fact, I don't even know why they did it."

She inspected the herringbone pattern of razor cuts on the inside of her forearm. Roman had painted them with iodine, a ritual that reassured her.

"The main thing as I see it," she said, "is that we're going to have to walk around here in shoes for a while until all the glass is picked up."

Roman shook his head in amazement. It had taken her thirty minutes to stop crying enough to talk at first. Now she was handling it as if it were a slip on the pavement. It was a show, and he appreciated it all the more.

"You know, I wouldn't have even noticed the hair that was pulled out," she said and rubbed her head. "I thought it was just part of the overall headache. Does that make me a poor victim?"

"Lousy." He watched the smile on her face disappear. "What's the matter?"

"The reason they didn't do anything to me. Except scare me to death. They wanted you, to kill you."

"Well, they missed and got you, and it's my fault. I'm not going to leave you alone like that again, I swear. There's a police sergeant who owes me a favor. He and I will find out who these . . . people were."

"No." Dany grabbed his arm. "They won't come back. Forget about them. I'll look through the peephole and won't open the door without the chain on from now on.

Please. If you want to do something for me, don't do anything. You don't know how much it scares me when you talk like that."

"Okay. Okay." He patted her knee. "I'll just let the cop do his job. How's that?"

Dany was relieved. He'd never given in to her before. She threw her arms around him and kissed him.

"Wait, wait a second. You have to tell me what to tell my friend." He thought the ordeal might be too upsetting to relive, but Dany had no qualms about talking, like a child who's only afraid of the dark when he's alone.

"I can't remember exactly what they said. I was too scared," she admitted. "All I know is that I think there were five of them, and I think two were men and three were women. I can't say how big or little."

She spoke for a long time without adding much in the way of facts. She'd been blind and terrified and usually dead to the world. One thing she felt was an impression that they had come for one thing, to get Roman, and without him they were vaguely at a loss. The destruction had been vicious and general, although there was something about china that she couldn't remember. And the safe, they hadn't been able to get into the safe.

When her eyelids drooped, Roman brushed the crumbs off the bed and laid her head down on the slashed pillow. He turned the lights out, and as he walked back to the bed, he dropped his clothes on the floor. This was one time when they wouldn't make a difference. When he got into bed next to her, Dany moved her head from the pillow to his shoulder.

"It's a funny thing," she said sleepily. "Just goes to prove how dumb I am. When I woke up the first time after he held my nose, I kept thinking how hot they were in their ski masks, and how nice it would be for us to go skiing. You'll have to take me to the White Mountains."

She was asleep by the end of the sentence. Her hair brushed over Roman's mouth. He had never been more awake.

He hadn't told her what he found as he searched the apartment. The blood and hair had not been taken for no reason at all. They were necessary for the image, the little broken warning that he looked for as soon as he saw what they'd done to her. It wasn't hard to find. In the wreckage, the untouched case stood out like any lone survivor. It was a small custom-designed chest about a foot high, made in Philadelphia about 1750 for the various eyeglasses of a wealthy buyer. Franklin's bifocals were not popular yet, and the case had drawers enough for six pairs. The drawers and chest were made of cherry wood, and the inside was lined with velvet.

In the first drawer he pulled open was a tiny pink leg. He recognized it as coming from a porcelain Victorian doll in his collection. The leg had been ripped from the hinge. It was wrapped in one of Dany's hairs and smeared with her blood. He took the other leg from the second drawer, the torso from the third, the right arm from the fourth and the left arm from the fifth. The head was in the top drawer. Each of them had been similarly tied and painted,

The callers had left another memento, probably less intentionally. The scarf they had tied Dany up with was an unusual one. It was a long, thin braid of black silk, and one end was tied around a gold four ducat with the placid profile of Franz Josef. He was not surprised that it had cut off her circulation.

He patted Dany's sleeping, content head. It wasn't so dumb of her to wake up thinking about skiing in the White Mountains. After all, that's where Hillary Sloan and her friends were heading, according to the brown spotted piece of map he found next to the doll's head. He didn't have to accept the invitation, the doll said, but then Dany would take his place.

18

Roman entered New Hampshire on the F. E. Everett Turnpike outside Lowell. He felt respectable just using a road with a name like that.

"You should be happy. You don't sound happy at all," Isadore had said on the phone from Boston. "The agent admits he didn't look in the chest. The girl's blood matches the type on the chest and the saw in Sloan's workshop. Sloan has no, repeat, no alibi." He was upset when Roman told him about the visit to his apartment. "I'll get onto it as soon as I get back. As for the murder, though, the only possibility is that they saw your name in the paper. Captain Frank gave everything but his mother's maiden name to the press. You and Lippincoot were called consultants. Didn't you see the papers?" Roman let Isadore in on the fact that he didn't read the papers. "Well, the kids do," Isadore said, "and you know how it is. One weird case like this sets off a whole army of kooks. It's not revenge, I'll tell you that. Sloan didn't have a friend in the world. Would you believe this guy turned out to be a forger?" Roman said he was shocked. "I'll bet. Sloan is almost as upset about that as the murder." Roman asked whether Isadore could drop everything he was doing and join him on a trip. "You're crazy. You don't know what you're asking. I know you're upset about last night, and I'll do everything I can. No, I can't spare any men either. This isn't my jurisdiction up here, and New York is still up in the air over politics. Just wait until I get back. Look, Sloan's new lawyer just ran in looking like his coat's on fire. I'll call you back." Roman accepted Isadore's excuses but remarked that, as a consultant to the police, he'd suggest that the sergeant look at the rings left on wood by a rotary saw. The same saw would leave anything but clean cuts on flesh. He also suggested that Isadore go to the library branch where the Mueller girl had worked and look up the records on readers who had taken out an unusual number of books on Gypsies and Indian mythology recently. "Leave the crimes to me and I'll leave the fortune-telling to you," Isadore suggested. Roman could hear two other men talking to the sergeant at the same time. One of them was Sloan's lawyer, and apparently he'd shown the Boston papers to Sloan, and Sloan did read the papers. "Hold it, hold it, Roman," Isadore shouted. "You didn't tell me you were at Sloan's house." That was when Roman hung up.

He felt better than he had in a week. He was free of promises and cooperation. A motorcycle passed as he gladly made room for it. The kids had been passing him all morning on cycles and cars. Many flashed the peace sign at him, and he returned it. Past Concord, he slowed down for a roadblock. State troopers were checking every bike and car. One with sunglasses motioned Roman to drive off the road; but when he started to, the trooper motioned him impatiently to get moving, and he saw through the rearview mirror that the center of interest was a large cycle. The troopers made the riders get off and stand for a frisk. They were looking for drugs.

The land changed to mountain country. A month later an older generation would tour it for the foliage. No troopers would wave them down as instant suspects. Sloan's lemon station wagon would have been undisturbed; now that sort of life was ended for him no matter what happened.

The traffic slowed down again. There was no roadblock,

just too many cars for the two-lane road. It was fifteen miles to Moultonboro, a small town on an isolated plain in the Ossipee Mountains. The rock festival started the next day on the plain between Moultonboro and the smaller town of Sandwich. The road was full of kids, driving and walking. A couple with a little boy and girl on their shoulders were moving particularly slowly, and he pulled over to give them a lift.

"Fantastic. Thanks," the guy said. The girl was in the back with the children and silent. It didn't make Roman nervous, but the young man shot inquiring glances backward.

"It's the car, not you," he whispered to Roman. "Pollution. She wouldn't have got in, but the babies were tired."

"Stop whispering!" the girl shrieked, "That's what I mean by male chauvinism."

"You whisper with your friends," he said meekly.

"It's the traditional right of slaves to whisper," she said. "Every time I think your sensitivity is heightened you go off getting palsy with some strange man."

"He's giving us a ride, honey." He leaned over the seat to talk to her. It was as if Roman weren't there to hear them.

"Honey! My name isn't Honey, buster."

"The kids."

She told him what he could do about the kids. The rest of the ride to Moultonboro the car was as silent as a tomb. When he left his riders off outside town, the guy stuck his head in the window.

"Guilt is a terrible thing," he said.

Everyone who was coming to the festival seemed to have already arrived. The plain north of Moultonboro was crowded with tents and, from what Roman could see from the makeshift parking lot, the heads of people weaving their way through the tents searching for their own square foot to spend the night. Far away the band platform was being assembled. Half built, it looked like a gallows. An attendant rushed up to take ten of Roman's dollars. The producers of the festival said they were expecting more than two hundred thousand spectators. It didn't look as if they were going to lose any money.

An encampment of Romany blended in with its setting. This camp overwhelmed it. He could see kids everywhere. A ripple from the fifties' baby boom rose like a multi-colored bathtub ring on Ossipee. The ground was beaten grassless and dusty. It was not only another nation but another world, one without shirts, with scarves, without combs, with leather armbands, a high distaste for the money system and more expensive 35mm cameras than he'd ever seen in his life. They were appealing more to him all the time. The fact that they were beating the ecology of the plain to death with their bare feet would have gladdened the heart of the blackest cynic. The flaunting of naked bodies was against every custom he grew up with. A Rom would never even indicate to his family that he was going to the bathroom, sexual lines were so strict. But there was an exuberance to these children struggling to break away from their *gaja* life-style that had to be sympathized with.

Breughel would have enjoyed painting the scene of self-proclaimed peasants in their bell-bottom pants, leather vests, headbands and beads. The kids were a show in themselves, and they enjoyed the show, gawking and commenting at warpaint on faces and surrounding the hundreds of impromptu blanket bands. A disjointed music covered the field from guitars, Jew's harps, sitars, harmonicas, drums and sticks. The only thing like it Roman had ever seen was the great market at Marrakech, and just as in Marrakech, hawkers moved through the crowd loudly vending their selections of hash.

A girl bare to the waist stared at Roman, and he realized something was wrong. He stuffed his tie into a back pocket and threw his jacket over his shoulder. The crowd spilled over onto Route 25, and there the kids were racing underneath kites. Most of them were of the plastic variety. Some were impressive Chinese kites of battleship dimensions with brilliant scalloped tails curling behind.

The number of naked kids increased as he ventured closer to Squam Lake. The physiques of the girls were tributes to American nutrition. The boys, on the other hand, were in distressingly poor shape, and they resented Roman's presence more.

I had been happy if the general camp,
Pioneers and all, had tasted her sweet body.

Roman turned to face a thin, heavily made-up girl in a purple robe. On her shoulders was a brace that balanced in front a large tome of Shakespeare's complete works and in back a poster reading "Peace." Altogether, she bore a strong similarity to some of the kites he'd seen.

"Do you know what it is?" she asked. Her eyes were lost in a welter of mascara. He confessed he didn't.

"*Othello*," she said. "You look like Othello to me."

"But I don't feel like Othello."

"Wouldn't you like to try?" she asked.

When he looked back at her a few minutes later, he saw he was more right than he thought. A gust of wind had caught the poster and was driving her toward the lake. She was trying to get out of the brace, but it was plain she wasn't going to make it. Roman had the manners to look the other way and walk on.

Afghans, St. Bernards and Irish setters provided a homey atmosphere as they nosed around kids stoned on pot. A monkey passed Roman at his own level before Roman saw that it was standing on the head of a dwarf.

Even the confrontations when festival guards had to identify themselves seemed to be just another part of the show. A boy with electrified orange hair had violated a commune's stew, and a guard on a motor scooter stopped to escort him to the highway. Immediately a ring of a hundred people gathered, most of them with Nikons or Leicas. Some of them sported heavy movie cameras. The boy pulled his shirt on and the guard tried to comfort him, explaining there were still some things you couldn't do at a rock festival. The boy got more upset, and finally, when it appeared he would cry, he hauled off and slugged the guard in the face, A thousand people were watching the familiar pantomime by now as the two grappled in the dust. There were some shouts of "police brutality," but they were halfhearted. A car prodded its way through the spectators, and the boy was slung in the back.

"That wasn't so bad. Thirty feet of action," the man next to Roman said. He was a lean perspiration-soaked individual with a dark crew cut and a wrinkled sports shirt.

A film camera was balanced on a shoulder saddle. "Hell, they make you pay fifty dollars to bring the camera in, you want to get something in return."

He told Roman where the public phones were. Roman had to wait fifteen minutes in a line before he got to the phone, and then it took the operator another five minutes to get a clear line to Boston and another five to find Isadore.

"What are you up to?" Isadore demanded. "What's with this trip? I've been calling your place all day, and Miss Murray just knows you aren't there."

"I'd tell you, but I don't want the local constabulary on my back."

"Wait for me then."

"Too late now. It would take you too long to get here. What changed your mind?"

"Who said I changed my mind? We're still holding Sloan. It's just that what you said about marks interested me. It reminded me of something else, too. There were scratches all over the dash of Nanoosh's car. There was only one that looked familiar at all, round scratches that you get from one of those little magnetic saints. Did Nanoosh have one of those?"

"Of course. Wasn't it in his car?"

"Damn it. It was on the road, and we thought it came from the van. Now that I remember, though, there weren't any marks like that on the van. Then I saw it again. Roman, are you going to tell me where you are?"

"No, but I assume you're having the call traced. I've been timing it, and it's been three minutes, and the operator hasn't interrupted yet."

"Don't fool around, Roman. I never was happy about the way that roommate changed her story on Sloan. I think there just may be a connection between that and what happened last night. So if you think you know who those people were at your place, just tell me. At least, wait where you are for me to show up."

"You're stalling," Roman said.

"You're goddamn right I'm stalling."

He placed the phone gently on the receiver and walked back out to the festival ground for a second tour. Isadore didn't understand, and even if he did, it was too late. He was threatened, Dany was threatened, and even if both of them escaped, that left a killer running loose. He was happy for the first reason because that left himself loose to act. There was another reason, too. In a petty but strong way, it offended him that the *gaja* dressed their threats in magic. The devil's head and the bloody doll irritated him instead of cowing him. The *gaja* world was for combustion engines, bank accounts and profitable rock festivals. The other world, the one of the immaterial, of vampires and ghouls, was the Rom's unlucky birthright.

A group of kids shaved and dressed as lamas shuffled by with chants of "Om!"

Isadore needed evidence, he didn't. One look at Sloan was enough. The collection of antiques and snobbery was a wall against inadequacy. If he'd actually murdered a girl, he simply would have fled, not butchered and shipped her coolly in his own antiques. Isadore didn't know the evidence when he had it. The rotary saw would have bathed the workshop in blood if it had gone through the neck of a person whose heart was still beating, as the coroner claimed. Instead, the cuts had been made by a weapon without a point. There was only one knife Roman knew of like that, the *bhotani*, the executioner's sword.

The lamas did a slow sort of Mexican hat dance with their feet. They were a pink, soft lot with vacant stares. The excitement in the area came from what appeared to be a circus.

19

A clown in a startling jacket of patches walked on high stilts, juggling large, varicolored balls over the heads of the crowd. His face was painted with red eyebrows and a red mouth. He executed an about-face and strode back to a second performer on stilts. The other one had the same painted face and a court jester's outfit of a belled cap, curly-toed slippers and checkerboard jacket and leggings.

Roman worked his way to the front of the spectators. A chubby girl in a long peasant dress was juggling Indian clubs while two other girls kept time with small cymbals. From time to time one of them danced with streamers, turning herself around like a Maypole. The lamas didn't have a chance. They muttered an "Om" or two and went on their way, leaving the audience to the circus.

At the end of the music, the clown let himself fall forward off his stilts, tumbling and landing on his feet artfully. The much smaller jester was content merely to jump down. Before the crowd could break up, the jester explained that what they had seen was a troupe of jongleurs. The jongleur, he said, was an ancient and respected profession. During the Dark Ages, jongleurs not only entertained the nobility of the time but also served as tutors for their children. They were harbingers of news from the outside world and repositories of knowledge. It was the jongleur who kept the lamp of reason burning during the dangerous Middle Ages. Testament to this, he said, was the high number of nobility who left their castles to roam the land as jongleurs themselves. Richard the Lionhearted was the best-known example.

"This is the new Dark Age, a dangerous, ignorant time. So we have chosen to revive the profession of the jongleur as a most honorable and necessary trade. We too roam the land. First as entertainers"—here there was a rattle of cymbals—"and second as seekers of knowledge. Naturally, we are dependent on your generosity for what we eat and drink."

It was a charming and informative presentation, and when one of the girls came around with a peaked hat held out for contributions, Roman put in ten dollars.

"Nice dance, Hillary. What else do you do?"

He thought she was going to run, but she controlled herself.

"Sometimes I sing."

"I'll wait around to hear you."

Her friends had seen him. They weren't bolting either. The jester talked some more as the troupe prepared new entertainment for their audience. The clown pulled musical instruments from the front of a Volkswagen microbus that had been spray painted in psychedelic colors. Then he went to the rear of the bus to untether a billy goat that had been lazily chewing grass around the wheels. He led the goat to the center of the ring.

"The traditional pet of the jongleur is the goat. Pan, the symbol of fertility," the jester said. The girls struck their tambourines. The goat's ears perked up, and it stood on its rear legs. It walked awkwardly, its front hooves bouncing off its chest.

"To the superstitious people of the Dark Ages, the horned goat was the manifestation of the devil. You probably remember how in *The Hunchback of Notre Dame,* Esmeralda was arrested for consorting with Satan simply because she danced with her pet goat. For this reason,

Gypsies were often tormented by peasants of the time for training goats to dance, although, in fact, the Gypsies were as ignorant of supernatural secrets as their persecutors."

The clown jumped in front of the goat. He waved a painted wand, and the goat's eyes followed it, the horned head bobbing and its rear legs hopping to keep up with the baton. The jester forsook his spiel for a flute, and the girls sang a medieval air. It was pretty and earnest, and Roman could tell the kids watching accepted it as part of their own new world. When the song was over and the goat was being taken back to the microbus, the jester skipped into the ring. The girls roamed through the audience, and Roman was taking his wallet out when he received a jab in the side. It was the crew-cut cameraman who had been at the scuffle.

"Keep your eye on this. They do it every show." He pressed his hollow cheek to his eyepiece.

The big clown brought out a wooden bull's-eye nine feet across and set it against a tree. He stationed himself with his back to the bull's-eye, his arms and legs cutting the colored lines into quadrants, looking straight ahead at the jester twenty-five feet away. The kids emptied their pockets so they wouldn't be searching for change when the action began. The jester made a rambling speech overloaded with quotes. Roman paid no attention to it, fixing his eyes on the narrow fingers that played with a silver fan of knives. The girls returned, and the jester looked indulgently on the money they poured into a chamois sack.

"And now the last member of our troupe as I promised you: death." The jester toed a mark and let his weight rest on his back foot. He selected one knife from the rest. Roman could feel the crowd growing from the pressure on his back. With no more fanfare the jester's arm came forward and the knife appeared three inches from the clown's belt. The clown didn't budge. The jester chose another knife, weighted it and threw. It appeared two inches from the other side of the belt. Roman looked at the target's face. There was no anxiety. A third knife popped up next to his shoulder.

"Not bad," the cameraman commented. "Not professional but not bad." A boy next to them frowned for quiet. The cameraman gave him an obscene gesture and went on. "Of course, the knives are coming out from the back of the bull's-eye and the little guy is palming the ones he pretends to throw. An illusion, you know what I mean."

Roman had picked a spot halfway between the jester and the clown where there was a solid background of dark leaves. For an instant that was practically invisible he caught the flutter of a metallic bird. A new knife perched beside the clown's throat.

"You know these kids pretty well," Roman said,

"Hell, I see right through them," the cameraman muttered.

The jester raised his empty hands. The clown stepped away from the bull's-eye and did the same, if possible even more calmly than the jester. "They're so hopped up on drugs they couldn't. . . ." He described what they couldn't do, in detail.

"Thank you, gentlefolk," the jester said, "for your good vibrations and even more for your money." The cameraman spluttered an expletive of agreement. "See you tomorrow, and may hallucinations of sugarplums dance through your heads."

The girls drifted into the applauding crowd for a last donation. "See what I mean about drugs?" the cameraman said. He let his heavy machine slide off his shoulder and hang by a scrawny arm. His short-sleeved shirt had turned completely gray with perspiration. "Say, how'd you like to join me in a few drinks back in Sandwich. We could scare up some action, some groupies. The boys are all queer, but some of the girls aren't so bad."

"I see you're a married man," Roman said, looking at the ring on the man's hand. "It must be fun having something in common with your kids." He turned back and watched the clown pull the knives from the bull's-eye. The cameraman was flushed, but he couldn't read anything hostile in Roman's dark face because Roman had erased him from his mind.

"You know the trouble with you jigs," he said at last. "Nobody's good enough for you." When he didn't get a reply, he slapped a cap over the lens furiously and left, pushing his way through the departing crowd.

Hillary deliberately collected from the far side. The

chubby girl was near Roman. She had a timid smile and a heavy application of makeup. He put a fifty-dollar bill in her tambourine.

"Wow, thanks!"

The crowd had almost dispersed, and she waved the bill at the jester to get his attention. She blushed immediately, regretfully, but the jester had seen her and came over. He had one of the knives in his hand. He was thin, and his dark eyes moved over Roman speculatively.

"I thought you might want to contribute something," he said as menacingly as he could.

Roman smiled, although he was anything but happy. For a short while he hoped he was wrong and that the jester was the one he was looking for. The first threatening overtone destroyed that wishful thought.

"Oh no," the clown said. He'd eased his way through the last of the crowd without Roman's noticing. He stood, taller than any of them, with his arms out in a gesture of friendship. Roman saw evenly planed, handsome features through the red-and-white greasepaint. The clown pulled his belled cap off, and a mane of blond hair fell to his shoulders. He smiled as broadly as Roman, the red mouth curling in satisfaction. "Don't you know the correct greeting is *sari-shan?*"

Roman put on his own mask of delighted surprise. The clown motioned Hillary to join them.

"You're a friend of Hillary's. She told me about you," the clown told him.

"No," Hillary said. She tried warning Roman away with her eyes. "We met only once." The clown glanced at the jester and the plump girl, enough for them to leave and start gathering the props spread over the ground.

"Imagine, a real live Gypsy," the clown said. The first cloud of the day passed overhead, casting a shadow over the small circus. His blue eyes glowed in the sudden dark.

"And very superstitious," Roman added. He took in the ironic hilarity on the clown's face. He could imagine him without any difficulty slipping soundlessly into a second-story window. "Somehow I feel we've met before too."

"Don't you have to go back to New York now, Mr. Grey?" Hillary asked pointedly.

Roman ignored the question. "I've never seen a rock festival before."

"You'll miss it," Hillary said. "It's not until tomorrow. Now we have to pack up."

Roman smiled and watched the other performers gathering the colorful litter of props. The bright balls reminded Roman for some reason of the broken shells of a giant bird and the jongleurs of hatched, ungainly young. Hillary and the clown would be the beautiful ones, of course, the violent aristocracy. The rest were merely a chorus for whatever tragedy those two would make of themselves.

"It's not every day we get to talk to a man like Mr. Grey, Hillary," the clown commented.

"It's not every day I see such educational entertainment either," Roman said.

Hillary bit her lip. The clown laughed and winked at Roman as if they were in a male conspiracy. The force of personality came off him like a hum off a tuning fork.

"Hillary never mentioned that she was part of a traveling troupe."

"She's very shy."

"I suppose so. She hasn't even introduced us."

The two men waited until she said, "Howie, this is Roman Grey."

They shook hands. The clown's grip was as strong as Kore's. "No last name?" Roman asked.

"No," the clown said lightly. "No addresses or credit cards. Isn't that like Gypsies?"

"But we have many names. For ourselves and for other people."

"Secrets! I love secrets," Howie said enthusiastically. "Maybe you can teach us some."

"Mr. Grey was going, weren't you," Hillary said. It wasn't a question.

"Impossible. He came to see the festival, and he's a friend. He can stay with us tonight. Can you imagine it. Secrets!" The way he said it made the word sound itself like a secret.

"He wants to get home."

"He wants to see a real rock festival," the clown argued persuasively. His arm went around Hillary, out of sight.

Roman watched her pupils dilate with pain. "Don't you agree?"

"It would be interesting," she said slowly.

"Great, it's settled then, Just give me a chance to get this paint off, and we'll be going."

"Where?" Roman asked. "You never said."

"There," Howie said. He pointed to the lake. Roman saw a small, thickly wooded island in its center. Its reflection in the water gave it the shape of an amused mouth, and if it had been red, it would have been a perfect copy of Howie's. Roman really would have preferred his enemy to be the knife thrower, not the man who amiably waited for the knives without flinching.

20

Close up, the summer afternoon gave the island an inviting haze. An oar scraped rock, and Howie jumped in the water. It splashed around his knees as he easily pulled the boat onto the beach over a hiss of rocks.

"Ararat," Howie said. He stood on the beach, the rope held lightly in one hand, his weight on one leg, and he reminded Roman of nothing so much as Michelangelo's David with perhaps the curl of the lips a trifle more pronounced, the shoulders Americanized and broadened. He was dressed completely in pure white buckskin that reflected the sun.

The rest got out. Without his costume and paint, the jester was a thin boy with the large head of a prodigy. His name was Gerry, and he dressed in a flower shirt and bell-bottoms belied by his accountant-close haircut. The plump girl wore a waistless peasant's dress and a bow in her hair. Her name was Rosalind. Isabelle kicked at the water spitefully. She had an angular, heavy-cheekboned face, and her black eyes had the warmth of dead coals when she looked at Roman. Hillary stared back at the festival, the breeze towing at her gold hair.

"I'm so glad you came," Howie said earnestly as he

took Roman by the arm. "The others didn't think you'd show up, Hillary most of all. I said, if anybody would, you would. The girl wasn't too hurt, was she?"

"More frightened," Roman said. The others were hurrying to the camp deeper on the island. He and Howie followed slowly, like lifelong friends.

"Good. You don't know how much I admire you. You're what, ten years older than I am, but I related immediately to you. I am something of a student of Gypsies, and this is a real treat for me." The way to the camp was padded with moss. Bright orange salamanders watched them fearfully. "That's where I first saw Sloan and the girl together, you know, at the library. She kept a whole list of the new mysteries especially for him. That struck me as one of the twists, by the way, creating a mystery around a man who was such a devotee of them. Anyway, I saw him there"—Howie cocked his head at the memory—"and he saw me, too, but he didn't recognize me. Isn't that odd? I'd brought antiques to his place two or three times. That's how I met Hillary. But, see, he didn't recognize me because to him all people who looked like hippies were the same. He couldn't be bothered to separate them into individuals.

"This is what fascinated me. I could kill his girlfriend, and he still didn't suspect who could have created this mystery all around him. But with you, all I had to do was—what?—cast a shadow in the woods and you knew I was there."

"That was why Hillary was asking me all the questions, wasn't it?"

"Yes. That was the first time I got a good look at you. Hillary thought you must be from the police." Howie grinned. "Of course, after your fast exit on the horse, I told her how silly she was."

"And you went off to get your devil's head."

"Exactly." Howie laughed with delight. "See how much easier it is for people like us? I met a police sergeant on Friday. He was as far from the truth as Sloan. He will even convict Sloan for murder on circumstantial evidence, and neither of them will ever understand what was done or why, two men operating in the dark and never knowing the rules of the game. While you, in an instant, would know Sloan was innocent. That was why I tried to warn you off. After we read about your connection with the police, we had to get more serious."

"You knew I'd come alone."

"Sure. I know you pretty well."

Hillary and the others watched them come into the camp. The two men walked arm in arm. Gerry had a fire started. Isabelle was rooting through a pair of rucksacks for cans of food. Roman looked around for Rosalind and spotted her beside a tree. Tethered to it was another goat, a black one.

"Do you like it?" Howie asked with an expansive gesture. "This is how we get away from the maddening crowd. I haven't whipped them into a *kumpania* yet, but it's a start."

"It is still in the Tom Sawyer league," Roman said. Howie laughed appreciatively.

Roman caught a look going from Isabelle to Gerry.

"What do we do with him?" Gerry asked. His hand was frozen in the act of slicing kindling.

"What do we do with him?" Howie asked back. "What kind of question is that to ask of a guest? We invited him, and he came." He strode across the clearing in his buckskin with his arms wide.

"We treat him like a guest," he said with a touch of humility that was so good even Roman was tempted to believe it. "He's one of us, an outsider. We should all stick together. Do you know how much you owe to the Gypsies? The rhymes, the songs. How many children's fears have been handed down by them." As he looked around, his long hair swung. He put a finger to his nose.

"Take this, for example. 'Hickory dickory dock.' You know it. 'The mouse ran up the clock. The clock struck one and down he run. Hickory dickory dock.' That's an old Gypsy rhyme that actually went, '*Ekkeri akkery an.*' It's a counting ditty. And there are many others, aren't there?"

"You're too generous," Roman said. "Hillary, are you the hostess?"

"I guess so," she said without enthusiasm.

"Like before."

She paled.

"At your father's house, I mean."

"Oh. Oh, yes," she said.

"No, not like then," Howie said. "This is fun. We all know each other now. We'll have a picnic and then some entertainment. First you entertain us," he said to Roman, "and then we entertain you."

"How is he going to entertain us?" Rosalind asked ingenuously. Roman had reached the opinion she was partly retarded.

"With the best kind of show," Howie said. "He's going to try to escape. You don't think he came here deliberately to get his throat cut, do you?"

He came up behind Roman and slapped him on the back. Roman was struck again by how handsome Howie was, not only the features seemingly cut from flawless marble but the same cerulean blue eyes of a statue. So when he smiled, the effect was ghoulish, like seeing a statue smile.

"What's it going to be? A little fortune-telling? Divide and conquer? I wonder if you can tell what we have in store for you?"

"The fortune-telling comes later," Roman said. "My medium works better on a full stomach."

"Beautiful."

"Roman, don't. It's not funny."

Everyone looked at Hillary. A gelid quality glazed Howie's eyes for a moment. Gerry coughed nervously and mentioned something about food to fill the silence. It snapped Howie back.

"Right, food. I've had to do all the work so far. Now I've got someone who can really help me."

"Gerry's pretty good with knives," Roman said.

"With still targets. I taught him how to do that," Howie said. "But hunting with a Gypsy, that'll be a kick. Of course, we won't be able to give you anything sharp, you understand."

"I somehow imagined there was a condition like that."

Gerry glared at him anxiously, long enough for Roman to grasp Isabelle's violent hate.

"Great, then we'll all go and watch. It'll be just like Mr. Wiz—"

"Howie, I don't think I can come," Hillary said.

Howie took a deep breath. "You'll come," he said in a voice that was almost different from the one Roman heard before. "You'll all come."

The salamanders scurried from the damp moss into the filigree shadows of ferns. A daddy longlegs moved giraffe-like down the bark of a beech. Roman and the jongleurs moved in single file past their tiny spectators down to the lake again. Hillary brought up the rear. Howie didn't mind; he was in good spirits again.

"And Kaliban, there's another Gypsy who never got his due. Half man and half beast. He only had one talent, he knew how to curse. Isn't that so?"

"You did spend a lot of time in the library," Roman said raising an eyebrow.

"And here we are, Kaliban. The vast deep, full of sea changes. What are you going to show us?"

They came out of the woods a little down from the boat. On the faraway bank the mass of kids played at shepherd like Marie Antoinette. In between, a trail shimmered on the water from the sun.

"Fish are usually what you find in water," Roman said.

"But the word is *matcho*," Howie said. "*Matcho*, fish. This is a good chance for the rest of you to learn the oldest living language in the world." The others spread out over the shore watching, except for Hillary, who squinted at the sun. "Without a hook, remember."

"I'll try."

Roman walked along the shore until he found a flat rock jutting over the water. He squatted on it and rolled his sleeves up.

"He's going to do it with his bare hands," Rosalind said excitedly. Gerry told her to be quiet.

Roman lowered his hands in the water. It was late in the afternoon but still hot. Beads of sweat slid down his cheeks. His hands descended at a rate that could be noticed only if one of those watching looked away and then looked back. It took five minutes in all. An underwater plant caressed the back of his hand. He waited another five minutes as the people on the shore became edgy. Something nibbled at a finger, and he felt the stiff bristles of a sunfish. The sunfish left as something bigger chased it from the shade. Roman hoped the others could keep still long enough. A smooth back grazed his palm. The trick was not to grab too fast or too slow.

"He's got one," Gerry shouted. A bass flipped on the ground, squirming in the dirt. It had lost its dark glow in dust by the time Gerry pushed his knife through the gills and began sawing the head off.

"Howie's got one, too," Rosalind said.

Roman had been too busy concentrating to see Howie wade into the water. He had his eye on a catch, too. Suddenly his arm was in the water. It came out empty. The knife in his hand was pink, though.

"You missed," Gerry said as Howie waded back.

"No, I got him."

When they left the lake, the headless fish in Gerry's sack, none of the jongleurs looked very happy.

"It was a joke," Hillary explained.

"That's right," Howie said as he walked with Roman. "I don't want to do any of the work for you," he said confidentially. "You've always heard of a man digging his own grave. But a man getting his own last supper, that's a little different."

"It shows imagination."

"Oh, you're humoring me, you dog you," Howie said good-naturedly. "I can see how you put Sloan through the hoops. Frankly, I think we have a lot in common. I even wish we could meet in different circumstances."

"Maybe we will," Roman suggested.

"That's the spirit."

Roman showed the jongleurs how to reap food from the island as Howie stood by and named almost everything they found. Wild onion, *purrum*. Watercress, *panishey shok*. *Pedloer*, nuts. Roman agreeably supplied *yakori bengeskro* for elderberries. All the time, Hillary fell farther and farther back. Once she had to go off by herself and be sick.

"Are you going to keep up with us?" Howie asked when she came back.

"I can't," she muttered.

"We can turn back now," Roman suggested. It was the last thing he wanted to do.

The marble lids clicked over the blue eyes once. "We'll go on. It doesn't make any difference."

Roman led the others through the woods, picking up speed gradually as Howie and Hillary followed. The forest changed from lowland woods to pines. The moss stopped, and a cover of pine needles began. Above, the sharp green tips tilted to the east. The incline became steeper, and he hurried because he saw ahead of him what he'd been searching for, the top of the island. Gerry and the girls scrambled after him with their sacks, but while he moved effortlessly through the trees, they kept slipping on the needles underfoot. They were relieved to see him stop on a bare knoll. Then they saw Howie with him. Somehow he had outdistanced them all.

Roman looked around. The whole island was spread out below a ring of pines.

"What do you think you're doing?" Howie asked sadly.

"Did you ever hear the old story about the man Beng took to the top of a high cliff and offered all the gold in the world?" The island fell away in stages to the west. Near the west shore were the burned remains of a house. South, a stand of birches like washed-out graves lay between the pines and a swamp.

"That's not a Gypsy story."

"Nobody said it was." There were no other campfires besides their own. No boats that he could see. East, there was a bare patch past the pines and then the sycamores and dogwoods around their camp.

"I could kill you right here," Howie said matter-of-factly.

"You could. I don't think that's what you want." He inhaled the pine resin deeply.

"What's going on?" Gerry asked as he reached them. The girls with their sacks of herbs looked as if they were on a real picnic. Their cheeks glowed with exercise. Howie was about to answer when a cardinal that had waited in the pine beside him until its heart was bursting shot out of the tree. It headed for the swamp: fluttering like a red handkerchief.

"*Chericlo*," Roman said. He left the knoll for the long slope going west.

"Bird," Rosalind said and followed with the others.

Howie waited for Hillary. She was just reaching the top, her hands against her sides. "You're slowing me down."

"I can't go any faster."

"You're always slowing me down."

Hillary watched him decide what to do. Obviously, he was considering a great number of alternatives.

The trail set below wound through a maze of pines. V's of brown needles kicked up over their feet as they followed the stocky agile figure in the lead. They caught up where he waited for them on a rock shelf. The pine forest had precipitously ended, and they looked out over a different, leafy woods.

"I never knew there was so much on such a small island," Gerry said.

"Look," Roman pointed to a gray shadow. Two ears twitched, and it was a rabbit. "That's *kaun-engro*, which is cleverly translated as the thing with the big ears."

"Can we catch him?" Gerry already had his knife out.

"I doubt it, but we can try."

The rabbit bounded to the side, and they followed on the ledge. Roman took the lead as the ledge became hemmed in by pines. A second outcrop of granite rose at its back, and they were forced to move sideways, looking straight down to the twenty-foot drop. Roman thought they'd have to back up when the ledge vanished, but he found it went around a bend in the outcropping.

"This would be a very good time for you to take off, wouldn't it?" Isabelle said.

Roman looked at Gerry, who said nothing. "After you," he told Isabelle and squeezed himself against the rock enough to let her pass. She went first around the bend.

Her hand came back and grabbed Roman's. When she was steady, he went around the bend with her. The rock ended at a seam of dirt and a sinkhole. Isabelle had almost fallen in. "There's a moral here someplace," Roman said. They edged their way between the wall at their back and the hole. It was ten feet deep, and the bottom was dotted with animal droppings. In the lower woods was a badly rotted line where a tree had fallen.

"That was here once," Roman said. He looked up. There were two large pines directly overhead on the upper rock. "The animals have taken over now."

"Snakes?" Isabelle asked.

"They prefer rocks, and they don't leave droppings like

that. More like pigeons. It would be a fox or a rabbit. Wait a second."

He went past the hole to the rock shelf on the other side. The granite had hundreds of crannies filled with small plants. Roman used them all to get down to the lower woods. Gerry watched anxiously, but Roman didn't have the cold sweat that warned him of Howie's presence. He tamely inspected the side of the shelf below them.

"Great, there's a small opening here. From the prints I'd say we have—"

"Say it in Gypsy," Rosalind urged.

"I'd feel safer if you were more explicit," Isabelle said.

"Hedgehog. Those who want the Gypsy version can see me after class." He had Gerry toss down a book of matches. "I'm going to start a fire with some brush and smoke them out. Use the sacks to catch them. Try not to knock each other into the hole."

The operation wasn't a complete success. They were half-blind from smoke when the hedgehogs finally came out, which was all at once and in all directions. They were lucky to catch two. Gerry was better at dispatching them.

As they walked through the lower woods to the black timbers Roman had seen from the hill, some change had taken place in the jongleurs. They carried their sacks with enthusiasm. Isabelle had stopped fixing Roman with blank stares. The larger change had been in him. He strode over the grass floor happily. His chin had a blue hue of stubble, his shirt was dirty and minus a button, and his hair hung in ringlets. He whistled a spirited *djili* to set the pace. Tiny emerald leaves of ivy crawled over the burned house, and a new sycamore was growing out of the enriched ground.

A margin of lilacs marked what once was the lawn. Rosalind ran ahead with a yell of excitement, swinging her sack. The rest trotted after her. She stopped before they did, staring up at the house, and then they halted in their tracks.

Howie stood in front of the black wall, an exclamation point all in white. The wind hardly bothered his hair, although the ivy behind him shuddered delicately.

"The picnic is over," he said,

Roman was the only one to take the last few steps up to him. "It's hardly begun."

Howie tilted his head back to the sky. "Getting dark. God, they're long, aren't they?"

"What's long?" Gerry asked.

"The days," Roman said. There were, after all, moments when he understood Howie in a way the others couldn't. The moon had risen in the still bright sky like a ghost. "There's one more thing. Here."

He went down into the gutted cellar of the house. The cement floor was an inch deep in water at places. He went to the part hidden under the shell of the first floor. Everything he touched left a blur of soot. He found what he wanted in the darkest, innermost corner of cement and beams. He killed it before it woke up.

They watched him come out of the cellar. Gerry had his knife drawn, but Roman's hands were together. He drew one away to reveal a crumpled ball of fur, leathery wings and a face that was mostly flaring nostrils. Howie pulled back the lid of its left eye. It was missing.

"What does that mean?" Gerry said.

Howie sighed. "It means that the man who has it has the power of invisibility."

"I still see him."

Howie's blue eyes scanned Roman. "Now I really see him."

21

The fire sprawled redly through its border of rocks like lava in the dark. A few of the hardwood skewers had dried out and added to the blaze while bones made irregular shadows in it. A pot, empty of soup and askew, reflected the glow. Roman lit a Gauloise in the flames and blew out a long plume of smoke.

"A last cigarette," he said. "What a nice tradition."

"It is about that time," Howie agreed.

"You didn't eat anything. Neither did Hillary."

Howie didn't answer. He looked at his hands, held out in front of him. They were large and strong, but there was nothing brutish about them. They were almost hairless. He lifted his eyes and watched Roman. Everybody else was.

"What is death like for a Gypsy? *'Ban, ban, Kaliban?* Has a new master, get a new man?' "

"You're asking the wrong Gypsy. Ask Nanoosh."

Howie was momentarily puzzled. "Oh, the Gypsy who died in the crash. But we only have you, and that won't be for long." His voice was sad, but his face was as empty of emotion as a mask. "I think you're out of secrets."

"The entertainment, I'd almost forgotten," Roman said. "The least I can do."

"Fortune-telling?" Isabelle asked.

"He's kidding," Gerry said.

"He's serious," Howie said. He clapped his hands together.

"He's going to try it. Come on, Kaliban, *duikker* for your life."

"Where's his crystal ball?" Rosalind asked.

"He doesn't need one," Howie said.

"Not now," Hillary said. "This isn't the time for card tricks or jokes, please."

"Quiet, quiet in the audience," Howie said. He stood up and strode back and forth as he talked. "Ladies and germs. Hah-hah. Tonight only an appearance by royal command. A chance to gaze at the hand of fate, to pick a card from the deck of tarot, an opportunity to reach back in the past or forward into the future. Who will be the first to tax the mental powers of the victim? Pardon me, sir, the mæstro. Yes, the chubby girl in the back row."

Rosalind put her hand down. She tried to look as cunning as she could as she posed her question. "How did Gerry meet Isabelle?"

"They're brother and sister," Roman said.

"Very good, very good," Howie said and led the clapping. "Not a toughie, but he fielded it pretty well."

"How did you know?" Rosalind asked. She was impressed if nobody else was.

"Gerry is her younger brother, and she's always had to look out for him. That's why she wishes I were already dead"—he shrugged—"so I couldn't show up here. She loves him."

"He embellishes," Howie announced.

"Let's try something a little tougher than that," Gerry said. His face was red, not only from the heat of the fire. "You tell us about Judy Mueller."

Howie didn't say anything. He squatted in the shadows and watched Roman attentively. Rosalind's head jerked toward the goat tied by its tree. It was still there by the evidence of its orange minus-sign eyes.

"The girl. I can't tell you much about her life. I'd guess

it was pretty dull if she could fall for your father, Hillary. No offense, I hope."

He lit another cigarette. "Howie would say that the only extraordinary thing about her was her death. He wouldn't be wrong. She was surprised, but then you all were, weren't you? Except for Howie. You thought it was a joke. You were going to scare her off so she wouldn't marry Mr. Sloan. So you took the yellow station wagon and honked the horn. Howie, you followed them before, so you knew what to do. She got in, and you took off. Hillary was along, so she wasn't scared.

"You took her into the woods. The whole thing was going to be a prank. You were all walking along. Nobody was holding her hands, nothing. Suddenly, from nowhere, Howie cut her head off. The rest of you stood around, not saying a thing, while he took her clothes off and chopped her up. Then, just in case you thought it was a whim on his part, he brought out the plastic bags, and he told you, Hillary, that your father was sending some things down to an antique show in New York. He'd know.

"Well, you know all the rest, but there was one thing about Judy Mueller you didn't know. She'd thrown your father over, Hillary. You didn't know her as well as you thought. You didn't have to kill her; she didn't have to die at all."

There wasn't a sound when he finished until Gerry said, "You're lying!"

"High marks," Howie said,

"You made it up," Hillary said.

"It was in her letters to your father. Of course, if you and he had had communication, you would have known."

The revelation had been lost on Rosalind but not on Isabelle. Her black stare covered Howie.

"That's over, though. She's dead, and you can't bring her back," Roman said. "Isn't there something you'd like to know about the future? Something happier than all that?" He looked around. They looked in a state of shock. "No? How about you, Hillary? Wouldn't you like to know if you're pregnant?"

Her eyes reminded him of the horse before he bolted.

"Come on, this is just after-dinner entertainment. The

Gypsy's last act. Howie must be curious himself by now. He's the father. Right, Howie?"

Howie hovered in the shadow, a suspended mask.

"Go on," he said.

Roman had Rosalind give him a tambourine from a sack. He used a charred skewer from the fire to draw nine lines on it, three descending like ladder rungs down the middle, the others describing a broken circle around them. He picked a handful of stones off the ground, selected nine and threw the rest away.

"Let me explain first that we should be using beans but . . . ah, well." He put the stones in Hillary's hand. She let them fall, but he caught them in the drum. "If they stay within the lines," he said, "you are. And if they don't, you aren't. You'll excuse me for skipping the mumbo jumbo." He tapped the bottom of the drum with his fingertips. The stones danced with a life of their own. He felt the suspended breaths around him. He gave the skin one final tap and stopped. The stones came to rest, all nine of them inside the lines. "Congratulations."

Hillary didn't say anything.

"You are pregnant?" Isabelle said.

"That's great," Gerry said. Howie didn't reply, and the burst of enthusiasm became strained.

"Would you like to know what sex it is?" Roman asked. "We can find out if you want. It's easy."

Hillary glared into his eyes as if he were a stranger. In a way, he was. His face glowed with a bronze wetness from the heat of the fire, and his thick black hair was coiled. With his shirt open, she saw a seashell hanging on a cord over the black hair of his chest. His eyes were lined with red.

"It would be fun," Rosalind said.

"Have you got an egg in one of the sacks?" Roman asked Gerry. Gerry said he thought so and took out a carton. He made a joke about breakfast and took an egg out. He gave it to Roman.

"Fine. Now, you have to hold this under your shirt against your belly for five minutes with the fat end toward you. Then we'll break it open at the other end. If the yolk shows, it's a boy. If the yolk doesn't show, it means it was attracted to the female growing within you, and it will be a girl."

She just held the egg in her hand, so he pulled her shirt out and placed her hands inside it. There was some flour and salt beside the fire that he had used for the fish. He had Rosalind give him some baking soda from a sack. Gerry asked what he was making now, but Roman silently moistened the flour and soda and salt. When it was soft, he brought the bat out of his shirt and sprinkled some of its blood on the dough. Then he rolled it into a strip and wound it around a stick and placed it over the fire.

"Okay, Hillary, let's see what you have." He pulled her hands out of her shirt gently and disengaged the egg from her fingers. He held the warm egg close to his face, waiting until Gerry's nervous coughing ended.

> *Anro, anro in obles*
> *Te e pera in obles,*
> *Ava cavo sastavestes!*
> *Devla, Devla tut akharel!*

He watched Hillary's pale eyes as he repeated it.

> The egg, the little egg is round
> Just as the belly is round,
> Little child come in health!
> God, God is calling you!

He struck the egg above the middle with a sharp stone and took off the cap of shell. He seemed puzzled, and he slid two fingers into the raw egg, searching. Hillary shook as he drew his fingers out, and after a moment when her mouth was open but mute, she screamed. Hanging from Roman's fingers, dripping with albumen and blood, was a small, hideous human head grinning.

"You dirty son of a bitch," Howie said.

Roman threw the head into the fire. The albumen crackled, turning first white and then black. The smell of hair rose out of the flames. Roman quickly drew the stick with the dough out. It had risen and curled around the skewer like a snake.

"It's an old trick," Howie shouted. No one paid attention to him. They had seen the head come out of the egg. Roman pulled the dough off the stick and gave it to Hillary.

"Eat some. It has bat's blood because the bat is the purest of all birds in that it suckles its young. You have to protect your own child."

She numbly took the dough and bit off an end. She chewed and swallowed and took another bite.

"Now, Howie, it's your turn," Roman said. "You have—"

If there had been more light than the fire, he might have seen it coming. All there was a flash of color that reminded him of the frightened cardinal and then a soft penetration that spread from the temple over his face and down to his body.

There was another howl that almost woke him up and a sense of being handled. It was the sound of crying that finally came through the fog and brought him back. The first thing he saw was the moon, no ghost anymore but a tangible entity. From its position through the leaves he knew he'd been unconscious for ten or fifteen minutes. His pulse roared over one side of his head. He expected that much; what worried him was that he couldn't move his hands. They were tied to his side and around something else. It wasn't a tree because when he moved, it moved. Then he felt the rough textured hair against his hands and a rank animal smell. He looked where the black goat had been and it was gone and he knew he didn't have to look any further. It was bound to his back, and from the limp way it followed his shifting body it was dead.

"He's awake," Gerry said.

They were still around the fire although from Hillary's face her mind was far away. Rosalind sobbed over the goat's collar. They all looked scared, except Howie. As he stood, a red scarf with a weighted end dangled from a pocket.

"You're very sensitive." Roman groaned. "Haven't you ever seen a devil's head before?"

Howie smiled in a new way; his beautiful head merely cracked for a second around the mouth. Roman rolled around until he had enough leverage to sit up. A sticky fluid ran down the back of his neck.

"Secrets, real secrets," Howie said. "No more of that *bajour* junk." He stood between Roman and the fire, his silhouette hiding objects that cast strange shadows over the ground.

"You had to kill the poor goat to tell me?"

"It's part of it. So is this. Recognize it?" Howie took something small from his pocket.

"It belonged to Nanoosh."

"Correct!" He held it up for the others to see. It was a plastic dashboard religious statue like a million others, but it was black. "His *Develeskie Gueri*, right?"

"The Black Virgin," Roman said. He tried sliding his hands out of their bonds. It was no good.

"What religion, Kaliban? Christian?" His voice boomed into the dark. "Isn't her name Kali?"

"There is a patron saint of the Gypsies known as *la Kali*," Roman said. "There's a pilgrimage for her once a year in France."

"Yes, at Stes.-Maries-de-la-Mer. There are Kalis, Black Virgins, in Poland, Portugal, at Chartres, in Czechoslovakia, wherever the Gypsies are. Through all the cities they have gone through, like Calcutta, Karak, Karachi, Carakalu. Isn't it true that there is another name for Gypsies besides Romany and that name is Kalo? Isn't that true, Kaliban?"

"Would someone please tell me what Howie is talking about?" Roman said.

"What are Gypsies, anyway?" Howie went on. "The Dravidians, the people who inhabited India before the Aryans. Reduced to becoming wanderers, untouchables, thuggees. To pretending that they worship this Kali"—he shook the plastic figure—"when the real Kali is right here."

He reached behind him and slammed down on the ground in front of Roman a statue two feet high. It was the representation of another black female but in a grotesque manifestation. Her breasts hung loosely under a green necklace of bodies and skulls. Around her waist she wore a belt of mutilated hands. Two of her many arms held up a demon's head and a broad-headed sword. Her teeth were tusks, and her forehead was marked by a third eye. Most striking of all, though, was her tongue, still glistening with the goat's blood.

"Kali!" Howie said. "Consort of Shiva. Her lust for blood grew from her battle with the demon Raktavira whose special power was that every drop of blood that touched the ground brought forth a new demon. She defeated him by drinking his blood as it flowed, creating a thirst that could never be satisfied. And a ceremony that demanded the death of a black goat and a man."

"The old stories about Kali and the thuggees?" Roman said. "The English wiped them out a hundred years ago. There aren't any more human sacrifices or men with strangler's scarves or executioner's swords."

"Then what are you doing tied to a goat, and what is this"—he drew the scarf out and threw it aside—"and what is this?" He reached back for the other hidden shadow and brought out a short crescent-headed sword. He sank it headfirst into the ground beside the idol. The fire's glow curled around its twisted handle of silver and bronze.

"That is an Indian executioner's sword, probably of the last century," Roman said as if he were appraising a Queen Anne side chair. "It is sometimes called *bhotani* because it is from the city of Bhotan. Other times it is called *bhowani*. Or Kali or the Black Mother. There are smaller versions in junk shops all through New York City, but it's difficult to find a real one. Where did you get it?"

"Thailand, while I was in the service. That's when I first became interested in Kali and you."

"Me?"

"That's how we were going to scare that dumb librarian, with the statue. I knew that wouldn't be enough. I knew everything was going fine when the cops gave me Nanoosh's Kali. They thought it was Buddy's." He paced behind the idol and sword, gesturing with his arms. "But you had to try to screw things up, and Gypsy or no Gypsy, that wouldn't do. So we had to hunt you, us and Kali."

"Interesting," Roman said. "An interesting theory. Let's say one or two facts are true."

Howie laughed. "You're in no position to talk about theories."

"Why not? According to you, Gypsies have worshiped Kali for thousands of years. What would you know in comparison to what I do? The names of evil: Mot, El-Zebub, Lucifer, Baal, Seth, Leviathan. Kali's names: Parvati, Uma, Gauri, Ambika, Durga, Chamundi, Minakshi, Devi." He looked at the others. "Does he know enough for your brother to become a murderer, Isabelle?"

"He's trying to save his life," Howie said. "He admits what I said is true. Kali is the goddess of destruction, the Clawed Hands, the Blood Drinker. This is her sword and that"—his hand, the fingers spread, reached toward the idol—"is her face."

"And that's one side of her, as it is for any god. If you knew her for thousands of years you'd know she could be all colors. The sky is black at night, but if your eyes were good enough, they could see the different lights of a million stars. Death is part of her because death is part of life. Was that your big secret, Howie? Maybe you can get that library card renewed."

Howie's eyes narrowed to shadows, and his hand fingered the butt of the sword. He gained control of himself, and the hand dropped.

"I almost forgot you were tied up," he said hoarsely.

"A worshiper of Kali, but you're afraid to kill me? Why?"

Gerry moaned and looked at Howie. Rosalind stared, mesmerized by the stubby sword. Roman spoke to them, trying with his voice and eyes to blunt the image of a bruised man tied to a dead goat.

"Howie surprised you when he killed the Mueller girl. There weren't any marks on her arms, so I know you didn't help him. The trouble was that you saw him do it. Now he needs you to kill somebody so you won't be witnesses anymore; you'll be killers, too. That's why he drummed up this story." The sweat poured over his face. In their eyes he glistened. "Let's see, I guess you're the man of the hour this time, Gerry. Then Isabelle, I suppose you're next to take a couple whacks. Then your turn, Rosalind. After that, Hillary, and then you'll dump what's left in the lake. If I hadn't shown up, it would have been some kid at the festival. That must have been something to look forward to."

"Not all of us can tell fortunes," Hillary said, breaking her silence.

"Everyone makes his future. All of us but Howie. *Te aves vertime mander, te yertil tut o Kali.* You have no future."

"You're threatening me," Howie said with amazement.

"She is." He nodded, and Howie followed the gesture to the idol by his side. Roman went on, completely without malice. "She does according to her wisdom in destroying what is useless or what has lived its destined time."

"There's only one person here who's lived his destined time," Howie said. He yanked the sword out of the ground and dropped the plastic statue in the fire. It bubbled, losing its shape and releasing a bitter odor. He watched with satisfaction and strode past the fire to the others.

"Now?" Gerry asked.

"We're not going to have any ceremony." Howie thrust the sword at him, handle first. "Here." He forced it into Gerry's hands and forced the fingers around it. "It'll be easy. One swing."

"I don't think I can do it," Gerry said. He seemed to be in physical pain.

"Damn it, get up. You don't even have to look. Just swing the thing and I'll hold him still. Get up." He grabbed Gerry and pulled him to his feet. Gerry looked at Howie in terror, and his knees folded. He dropped the sword as he hit the ground and curled up.

"You little twit, get up or I'll use it on you," Howie said. His rage was slipping away from him, reshaping his pale face. Hillary saw it. It was the face from the egg.

"I can't," Gerry cried.

"He's telling the truth," Roman said.

Howie's head snapped around. "Another trick?"

"Poison, another old Gypsy talent, remember? Some mushrooms I picked up during our outing. I dropped them in their soup. It'll hit them all if they try standing, a little later if they stay still, but all of them. They should get to a doctor as fast as they can."

Isabelle stood up. She took one step before she gasped and sat down, holding her stomach. She tried cursing Roman and couldn't do that, either. Howie snatched Rosalind off the ground with one hand. He jammed the sword in her hand and pushed her toward Roman. She collapsed near the fire. Howie ranted, going back and forth, kicking and threatening them. At last he gave up and stood in the middle of them, furious.

"The doctor," Roman repeated. "Unless you want three more bodies to dispose of. Now that could get tricky."

Howie pulled Hillary to her feet. Roman hadn't given her any of the mushrooms, and she wasn't sick, not physically at least.

"You do it," Howie yelled in her face. "He knows too much."

"He always did." She refused the sword and turned away to the figures on the ground. "They're dying."

A sound that was nothing less than a growl came from Howie's throat. He pushed her away and grabbed the nearest retching body. Roman stayed as still as he could. Howie was going to take them to the boat. He wouldn't row them across, but he would be gone from the camp for a minute or two. Even with a dead goat on his back that would be enough time to get away.

Howie watched him, reading his mind.

"It looks like I'll have to do it again all by myself. When I'm finished, when I . . . you and the goat are going to look like Siamese twins." Rosalind hung from one hand, and he picked up the idol with the other. "And if you want someone to keep you company until I get back, here's your goddamn Kali."

He threw the heavy idol as easily as a beanbag. Roman tried to turn to make the goat catch the burden of the blow. He didn't succeed. The idol smashed into his ribs, and he rocked, finally falling forward with the goat on top of him.

Out of the corner of his eye he saw the moon, cruelly cut by leaves. The moon began contracting, first to the size of a silver dollar, then a quarter and then a dime. There was no air in his lungs, and none was coming in. *Dude* was supposed to be good luck, he was sure of it.

On the other hand, he thought as the moon disappeared, there were always exceptions.

22

"Did you really poison them?"

"Enough to make them sick."

Hillary had rolled him on his side so that the goat's weight was off him. A draft of air poured into his lungs. Hillary's face was as faraway as the moon.

"Where are the others?" He was gasping so hard he doubted that she understood him.

"We took them to the boat. I ran back while Howie was putting them in."

He stared up at her because everything else but the fire and the moon was dark. She thought the startling eyes could see more, and she began pleading with him.

"Please don't kill Howie, You've got to promise you won't. I still love him."

"Kill him? I. . . ." There was something comical about her asking favors from a half-blind man lying on the ground tied to the corpse of a goat. The silent laughs scratched his ribs.

"He's coming back?"

"Right now, But you've got to promise that you won't do to him what you did to the others."

"Get them out of the way. So they wouldn't have to make a choice, choose." He wasn't making sense, and he struggled to get hold of his tongue. He couldn't afford to lose her.

"Promise?"

Promise? Everyone wanted him to make promises as if he had some power over the way things happened, him tied to Dany and Celie and a poor goat that was worse off than himself only by a matter of minutes. He fought the conspiracy of his ribs and temple and lurched up to his knees. The goat's hooves dangled in all directions like a bagpipe. Every time he moved the carcass sagged in a new place trying to drag him down.

"Help me, Hillary, for God's sake,"

She looked at him dumbly. He swore and repeated the plea in English. "It's a promise," he added.

Even standing bent over with Hillary supporting him, he was dizzied by the height. He really was Kaliban now, half man and half animal. He spread his legs cautiously, expecting them to fail.

"Untie me."

She seemed to notice his predicament for the first time. He almost collapsed as she fumbled with the rope.

"Would the sword help?" she asked.

"The sword?" He never thought Howie would leave the bhowani with them. "Of course. Where is it?"

"On the other side of the fire." It lay in full view only twenty feet away, reflecting the fire like a crescent-shaped mirror.

"Quick, get it."

Hillary hesitated, mildly curious why he hadn't seen it, and in that moment he heard Howie returning—not Howie returning because Howie moved silently but the unnatural vacuum of sound that precedes any predator. The katydids were the last to hush, and when they did, Roman pulled Hillary back.

"Forget it. Hold my hand and get into the woods, fast," he whispered.

Her slim white hand took his brown one and obediently led him away from the fire into the woods. Once among the trees he was totally blind. They were still within her sight of the camp when he abruptly knelt and pulled her down.

Howie stood at the edge of the camp directly opposite them. He was so motionless it was hard to believe that he hadn't been there all the time. When he moved, it was in long, unhurried strides to the fire, and he slowly looked around in a circle. Then he saw the sword. His eyes scanned the camp once more, and he noted the absence of the goat or the rope. He picked the sword up and laughed so loud Roman thought he could only be feet away. Hillary watched from the grass like a fawn.

"I know you can hear me," Howie yelled. "I know you're right here. You ran so scared you even forgot the sword, you know. You might have had a chance if you took the sword.

"Hillary, you made a bad mistake. I don't know how you think I'm going to take this, your betraying me like this. I'm not happy, you know that. Anyway, two of you are going to be a lot easier to find than one. The three of you, pardon me."

He laughed again.

"Can you see me? I bet you can." He turned quickly and relaxed again. "Hey, antique dealer, have you got any more tricks or did you run out? How's the bat eye working? A few words in Romany? No?"

Hillary started sobbing. Roman squeezed her arm until his fingers ached.

"Okay, play hard to get. It's all the same to me. But I think you'd like to see what I have in store for you two." He walked past the fire toward them. For an instant Hillary thought he saw them, but he bent to pick up the idol. He walked back to the fire with it.

"Gypsy, you watching? You too, Hillary. This is what I'm going to do with you." He held the idol out with one hand and brought the sword down with the other. The idol was made of hardwood, but the blade sank an inch through its chest and necklace. He pulled the sword out and dropped the idol. He attacked its head, slicing off the tusks and tongue and then, when it was on its back, began hacking away at its neck. The more he worked, the more furious he became so that when the idol was covered with gashes, his face was dripping with sweat. He wasn't satisfied until there was nothing recognizable left of the idol, no hands or breasts or legs, and then he stood exhausted with his hands hanging down, his face ash white, and stared at his victim. He picked up the decapitated head.

"What is he doing?" Roman whispered.

"He put the head in the fire, and he's still hitting it," Hillary said. Her voice sounded as if it belonged to a five-year-old in a distant room.

Howie slashed away until the fire and the head were indistinguishable, and then he went on cutting at the flames and slapping the broad head of the sword down so that there was less and less of the campfire all the time. At last there were only a few embers left, and he tracked them down, smothering them with the sword until they were all dead and, blow by blow, he had faded into the surrounding dark.

"Coming to get you."

They huddled as near the ground as they could get. Roman's ear was on the ground, but he couldn't hear a step. A cool breeze smoothed the grass around them, making them stand out as hillocks.

Howie would be on them now if he'd taken the right direction, and he had excellent night vision. No sword came down. The first insect began talking again. Roman took his hand off Hillary's arm. He wasn't surprised how cramped and sweaty his palm was.

"What do we do now?" she asked.

His map of the island was incomplete. The camp was on the eastern side, and he knew the land between it and the water. He knew the southern shore and an area between it and the island's high point to the west. They'd been through the pine forest and the woods to the house, but Howie had been very careful to lead them back to the camp by the shore trail. They center woods, the birch groves leading to the swamp, the swamp itself and most of the shore running from east to north to west were terra incognita.

"How well do you know the island?"

"Not well. I've been sick the last few days. I'm okay at night."

"Have you been to the swamp?"

"We picked some berries there." The timbre was coming back to her voice as she talked. "It's deep."

"We have to find some place to rest and get this off my back. Can you think of some place I didn't go today?" The swamp was out. Stumbling through it blind with no hands was just saving Howie work.

"No. We stayed in camp mostly. Howie was the one who went out and got food."

Roman closed his eyes to think. Having them open and seeing nothing was worse. They couldn't talk where they were for long, and when they moved, it had to be someplace in particular. Wanderers made noise. The south shore was the most logical path, and that, he was sure, was where Howie was waiting. They needed time as badly as Howie needed to finish quickly and make his escape. It was a long swim back to the bus.

"Hillary, do you know Polaris?"

"Of course."

"Can you see it?"

He felt her lean away. "It's that way. North."

They started off, Hillary following the star through the trees. She moved confidently, leading Roman by his shirt. It hadn't sunk into her that he couldn't see, and he knew it. Occasionally a tree would hit the goat and shake him; but the ground was level, and he kept his footing. Only once, they heard Howie calling out. He sounded so far away their spirits were lifted.

The ground became rougher, and Roman's feet scuffed against sharp rocks. A tall nettle reached his face and left minute red lines. Isadore might be at the festival; he might even meet the boat as it arrived. Roman forced the picture from his mind because it was wishing, not thinking. He tried pushing away guilt for the trick with the egg. That wasn't as easy. Hillary would have been safer hunting him than running with him, and now that he'd deceived her he would have to go on doing so. She was operating on lies.

"Look, isn't it beautiful," she said. They'd stopped. He heard the lapping of water and the amplified music of the kids traveling over the lake.

"See the Bear. And that's Cassiopeia on the other side."

Hillary looked up. Where Cassiopeia should have been was white cloud. She nodded happily.

"See if you can find a sharp stone," Roman said. He sank down and pretended to search the ground. Howie would have given up the south shore by now. Roman was sure that if he could get his arms free from his side, he'd be able to breathe normally. The moon passed between clouds and gave him an encouraging moment of sight.

"How's this?"

Roman told her to put it in his hand. He ran his thumb over the edge. It was glass.

"Great. Go ahead, cut the rope."

He leaned over and presented the bound goat. The ropes tugged his chest as she began sawing. It wouldn't take long for the glass to slice through. He listened to the whine of the mosquitoes busying themselves around the carcass. The short hairs on the back of his neck stood up; then all the hairs down his spine were erect.

"Hillary, are there any big rocks in the water?" She said there were, as calmly as if they were discussing a landscape.

"We have to get in the water. Don't make any splashes. Get behind the rocks and hide."

She immediately headed for the water without waiting for him. He managed to get hold of her belt with one hand and followed. The water rose to his knees and then his chest as she led him in. His face felt colder. The water's buoyancy made it easier for him to carry the goat and practically impossible for him to hide.

"How big are they?"

"Big enough."

There wasn't time to argue. The lake bottom fell away, and they were treading water. He lost his grip on her and regained it. A rock hit his chest, and he shouldered his way around it.

"See, here we are," she said.

He treaded as fast as he could. The goat, like an oversized hump, kept forcing his face into the water. He angled his hands up from his sides as much as he could and found a hold on the rock. When his shoe discovered a projection to rest on, he hugged the rough side of the rock as if he could get into it. Hillary was as composed as a sleepwalker.

They waited in the water for ten minutes while the chill

settled into their bodies. Then, before he could tell Hillary they were going back, a white birch moved in the bright moonlight from the other trees and onto the beach. It carried a shining branch over the spot where Hillary had tried to cut the ropes. As the white shape glided back and forth, Roman saw she had taken them only twenty yards into the water. The struggle to the rocks had felt like a mile when they'd hardly moved at all.

He remembered the ground when he'd pretended to search for a stone, a film of sand over rocks and hard soil. If there was more sand, the tracks into the water would be unmistakable. The apparition never turned to the water. It simply retreated and, bent over with the brilliant arm in front, dissolved back into the trees.

They waited another ten minutes and came ashore. Roman spit out the water he hadn't swallowed in the struggle back. The goat was twice as heavy as before. The ropes were tighter. Hillary hugged herself and shivered. Her dank hair hung over her shoulders, and her shirt was pressed over her breasts and belly.

"That was close. I'm amazed he didn't see us."

"Us? You don't have to worry," Hillary said, "you're invisible." She wasn't kidding. Roman's teeth chattered.

"Have you still got the glass? He won't be back for a while."

"I'm sorry, I lost it in the water."

The goat wouldn't budge no matter how hard she pulled. Finally, they started moving again only to stop and take off shoes that squished on the ground. She laced her sneakers neatly together and hung them over her neck to dry. In bare feet, they crept back into the woods, the girl leading what was at first sight a helpless beast of burden.

23

"The Bear is about five inches over the trees," Hillary said sleepily.

"Fine. Just three more hours until daylight," Roman said.

"Can I go back to sleep?"

"No, you'd better stay awake now."

The moonlight was bright and constant. The clouds were gone, and they wouldn't be back until dawn. Roman and Hillary were on the eastern fringe of the pine forest overlooking a meadow that ran to the woods in the center of the island. They'd been there for an hour, watching Howie move below. He was searching the island in a circular patrol that was tightening around the high ground. Each sweep was shorter. In the beginning there had been a fifteen-minute space between his appearances. It was down to about every five minutes.

Roman leaned forward. The rope was hooked over a stub on the tree, taking some of the weight off him. They'd never come as close again to freeing him from the goat as they had on the beach, but altogether they'd been very lucky. Twice Howie had passed within inches of

them, once in the birch stand when he'd suddenly mani-
fested again and once in the woods below. He was a smart
tracker. All of his screaming had been in the first hours of
the hunt, and he'd been patiently silent since. From Hillary's description, he stopped and took careful surveys
each time he came by. He'd know if there was something
different about a tree or whether a bush had exactly the
same outline.

Roman had him pegged now. The pure whiteness had
thrown him off just as the idol's blackness had confused
the others. Howie was Priculics. During the day, Priculics
was a beautiful young man. At night he was a huge black
dog that killed and devoured anything he met. He'd
hunted Faust, and now he was hunting them, padding
through the woods on all fours with his beautiful shining
teeth.

"Roman."

He shook his head. He'd fallen asleep. It was the strain
of trying to see when he could barely make out the blur of
trees.

"Roman, it must be wonderful being a Gypsy."

"Why?"

"You don't have to be scared of anything. I've been
afraid all my life. With you, nothing can happen."

"Shhh."

The white form slipped by sixty feet away. It was moving faster now. Howie's patience was wearing thin. When
he was gone, Roman and Hillary moved up to the next
line of trees. Moving over the meadow, they'd be too easy
to spot. Anyway, Roman liked to know where Howie was.

The search area was localizing around the knoll. On the
other side of it the pine forest ended in a cul-de-sac where
it fell off to the lower woods. Roman decided that they
would move in the direction of the knoll one more time,
and then they would have to make a break for it back
toward the shore.

"They're all asleep," Hillary said. The far shore was
completely dark; the kids had tucked themselves in. Roman wondered idly whether Isadore was wandering
around the blankets. "It's so peaceful, like the end of the
world," she said. "I don't mean destruction. I mean as if

their world ended over there and we had this island right off the edge."

"Finisterre."

"Right. And we'd make our own laws. Like we'd have things rise instead of fall and water could run upstream." She crouched next to his knee for warmth. "Is it silly to want that?"

"Everybody wants that."

She was answering him when he put his finger over her lips. The white blur was moving through the trees again, closer than Roman had expected. Hillary's body was close to Roman's, and he heard her heartbeat go from a placid rhythm to terror. Howie was looking up at them, studying the shadows inside the apron of branches. Something smaller moved down the hill like a bouncing ball. It was a rabbit. As the tall white blur moved on, Hillary stifled a laugh of relief. Her heartbeat returned to normal. Roman would have put his arm around her if he could. His sleeves and the front of his shirt were smudged with red where the ropes had rubbed the skin raw. She helped him to his feet, and they ran together to the next jagged line of pines. His back and legs were stiff from their cramped posture, and he moved gracelessly in her wake.

Hillary had just slid under the bows of their new hiding place when she screamed. The cry pierced the night like a bubble. Roman tossed himself beside her. A saw-toothed trap was shut on her foot. He recalled what she said about Howie leaving the rest of them in camp while he supplied food. That's what Howie had been doing all night, checking his traps. The teeth of this one had only closed over the toe of her sneaker. She took her foot out and left it hanging.

"I'm sorry," she said and hiccupped with fear.

"That's okay, but we have to get out of here."

It was too late. They saw Howie as soon as they crept out of the trees. He was running down from the knoll full tilt. When he saw them, he waved the sword and yelled unintelligibly. He approached as easily and mindlessly as the wind, his face lit by the moon with triumph. Roman and Hillary tried running downhill, but Howie caught up with them before they even reached their last hideout.

Roman, of course, was the first one he reached. Howie

brought the sword down with both hands on his back. Roman kept running and Howie struck two more times, the blade sinking deep into its target. Still Roman ran with his head down as the blows came down, almost jarring him off his feet. The crescent tip sliced over his head once, cutting off part of the goat's horn. Hillary hobbled far ahead on one sneaker, turning back up the hill. Roman fell to his knees and rose in one motion as Howie chopped and grunted in frustration. The face Roman saw was barely recognizable. Howie's lids were drawn back from bulging eyes, his lips stretched over his teeth. Roman tried dodging between the pines. Howie shrieked with pleasure and knocked him through the stiff branches, the sword flashing like quicksilver as it met Roman coming out. Roman's cramped legs started to give out and slip on the blanket of needles.

As Howie raised up for a final blow, Roman dived at his feet. Howie's swing had already started. It missed, and Howie went with it, plummeting face first. The needles rolled under him, allowing his hands nothing to grip. The sword spun on and on halfway down the hill before it hit a tree and came to rest.

Roman watched the disconsolate figure slide down the hill to gather its weapon. He saw the sword clearly, even its twisted handle of silver and bronze, as it lay in its cushion of needles. Howie took the sword away from the tree and stood looking back up the hill for the Gypsy without success. Roman saw him very clearly.

Roman started up toward the knoll. By the time he reached it his arms were free, and he was toting the goat over his shoulder like a sack. Once again the whole island lay around him. Howie was desperately climbing the hill far behind.

"You're alive." Hillary stepped from a tree timidly, afraid to believe her eyes. "You're alive," she said with more certainty. "He couldn't kill you. I saw it." She touched his face.

Roman unslung the goat from his shoulder. The carcass was nearly cut through, and one whole side was crosshatched with gaping slices. There was little bleeding because the animal was already dead. The ropes that bound it to Roman were cut through in several places. He rubbed his arms to encourage the circulation.

"Ouch," he said as he massaged a raw sore. It shook her, and he added, "I know I'm vulnerable, but even a Gypsy likes sympathy. Howie's going to be here soon, so we'd better go."

"Where are we going to hide now?"

"We've stopped hiding."

She wanted to ask what he meant, but he was leading her down the west slope of the pine forest. He continued to carry his grotesque burden. Not that it held them up. They had gravity going their way, and they slid on the seat of their pants through a rustle of needles. He led her through the dark maze as easily as if it were day. Once or twice she thought she saw a contented smile on his face.

The roller coaster ended when his arm shot out and grabbed her. Hillary skidded on her back to a stop. Overhead the pines were an angular wall bordering a blank sky.

"What is it?" She sat up and found herself on the edge of a rock shelf. Her feet dangled over a twenty-foot drop through the tops of dogwoods and sycamores.

"It's a part of the island you've never been to before. We don't run anymore. We face Howie."

"You mean we're in a corner."

"If you try to hide, that's where you end up; that's what corners and Finisterres are for. I should have faced Howie after I went to your house. I didn't. Well, Howie's coming down this hill any minute, and I'll have to face him."

"You don't seem very sorry."

"It's easier for me. You should split now. If things go wrong, you can hide until he leaves."

"I have to watch." She shook her head.

"He may get lucky."

"Howie doesn't have a chance. I always knew that."

He thought she was babbling about magic again until he caught the pinholes of pain in her eyes. She was talking about something he knew very little of, that he wanted to know nothing of.

"That's it then." He took her hand, and they edged their way along the granite shelf, dragging the carcass with them. Howie hadn't been along earlier in the day, but it was possible he knew the outcropping. Roman thought of the face with the sword and doubted that it made a difference. The fringe of a sycamore below touched their feet while the pines at their back tried to push them over. They moved cautiously until the higher shelf rose behind them. Ten feet farther on, the rock at their level curved around a dark void.

A short step beyond the curve brought Roman to the lip of the hole. His bare foot felt the roughness where Isabelle had almost fallen in. He located the eighteen inches of solid ground between the hole and the wall and stepped lightly to it. The hedgehogs, if they'd returned home, were silent.

Hillary took his hand, and he guided her beside him. There was barely enough room for the two of them, and she had to make herself as comfortable as she could in a niche in the wall. Roman stretched across her to reach the goat's rope. He pulled its carcass carefully between her feet and the hole to him.

"What are you doing?"

"Howie set a trap for us. We set a trap for him." He ran his hand along the rope. The part that had been cut into short sections he'd left by the knoll. Even the part he had was badly damaged. It only had to service once, he told himself. He tied a loop around the goat's shoulders and gave the other end to Hillary.

"Roman, remember your promise."

It seemed pointless after all the other promises he'd broken. Still, he said, "I know, that's what I'm trying to do."

He searched the granite wall at their back until he found a handhold. Hillary thought he must be climbing on air; but he moved quickly up the rock, and the next thing she knew he was asking for the rope. She threw it up. The goat began rising.

He worked fast, with an exhilaration he was ashamed of. He selected a strong branch for the gallows and tossed the rope around it twice. The free end of the rope he secured around the trunk of the pine. The goat lay on the ground under the branch and the slack rope. Roman checked the branch once more for snags and pushed the carcass out gently. As it cleared the upper rock, the body changing from horizontal to vertical over the lower shelf,

Roman played the rope out slowly, and the suspended goat sank until it hung with its hooves just inside the shadow of the hole. He secured it at that height with another knot at the trunk. He took off his shirt and used it as a muffle to break some of the smaller branches.

Hillary was near panic. She'd stopped thinking of the animal when it was on his back. Hanging beside her gave it human proportions, the warning of the overdone suicide. She fastened on Roman's whisper gratefully and took the branches as he handed them down. She thought he left, and then he was next to her again.

"You didn't tell me."

"You set a trap for what you want to catch," he said. He laid the branches over the hole, partially covering the dangling feet.

He tried judging the outline of the carcass. It sagged badly where the lower legs were barely joined to the body anymore. He covered the defect by dressing the animal in his shirt.

"I didn't think—" She caught her breath. The goat swayed and touched her leg.

"I know. Just stay as still as you can now. I'll come through first and then Howie. You don't have to do a thing. Here." He took something from his pocket and gave it to her. She knew immediately from the feel what it was.

"That helps."

Roman didn't have the stomach to say anything. There were lies and there were lies, and if she thought the bat's eye helped, she could have it. He steadied the goat and gave it one last critical appraisal. In the shadow of the pines all that would be visible would be a body with his shirt on.

"Thank you, Roman. I know what this means to you," Hillary said. He was gone, though. The clothed carcass jiggled beside her in the breeze.

The moon swelled and grew fat as it descended. The air became fresher, making the pine needles shiver as he moved up the hill to the knoll. Howie would be somewhere nearby because there'd be gore on the sword, and he'd think they couldn't go far. Roman made a complete circle of the knoll, and then he went to the top. The new wind was especially strong there, coming from the east. He settled on his stomach and waited. It wouldn't be long. Time was running out for Howie.

Howie was worried. It was obvious even at a distance. He was running back and forth where he had caught them. His mouth was open and gasping. Roman waited until the wind slacked off, then he started speaking just loud enough for his voice to carry. "Hickory dickory dock, the mouse ran up the clock."

Howie stopped and stared up at the knoll.

"The clock struck one, and down he run, hickory dickory dock."

Howie was coming up. Roman waited until he was fifty yards away, and he moved backward off the knoll. He swung down through the pines. He stopped when he could still see the knoll and started talking again.

"*Ekkeri akkery ukeryan, fillisi follasi nakelas jan, ekkeri akkery ukery an.*"

Howie's head appeared over the knoll, and then his shoulders. His blond hair was ragged with briars. There were dark circles under his eyes. He carried the sword low. During the long night it had become heavy. He looked warily around.

"*Hokkani hukkani dook,* the rat ran up the clock."

Howie saw him. The white figure crossed the knoll in two strides and came down the hill. He paid no attention to the trees, slicing at the branches as he plunged down in as straight a line as possible at the retreating man.

Roman twisted through the pines. He heard Howie fall and collide with a tree. Then the feet were following him again. He disappeared by cutting at a right angle from his path. The feet stopped. He let Howie get impatient for the voice before he spoke again.

"The clock struck one," the feet were sliding through the needles already, "and down he run, *hokkani hukkani dook.*"

Howie burst through the trees. Roman swung around a tree and ran to his left. Howie stumbled, swinging at him, but his fall carried him right behind Roman. Roman cut back to his right, sliding on his thigh. A branch separated cleanly by his head as Howie swung again. The sword began slowing Howie down. Roman gained a foot, then a yard, and Howie's thrusts became more and more futile.

Roman cut even more sharply to his right, and Howie fell, not able to grab a tree immediately because he was more concerned with holding onto the sword. Roman had completely disappeared. Howie stood up and leaned against a tree. This was an area of the island he'd never been in before. He took one step and held onto the tree tighter. Five feet in front of him was a rock ledge, and beyond that was nothing.

Roman stood on the ledge where the wall rose behind it. He waited until he was satisfied nothing had fallen into the lower woods. Then he repeated, *"Hokkani hukkani dook."*

Howie's head snapped around. The Gypsy was closer than he'd dared hope. He held the sword straight out at his waist and padded along the ledge.

Roman took five steps back. A pine needle cracked in the dark where Howie was coming from.

"Avata ratti dosch."

Another needle broke. Howie was becoming less anxious about being quiet. He saw the wall block the stone shelf off from escape through the pines. He hesitated because he didn't know whether Roman had taken the exit.

Roman crouched where the shelf curved. He couldn't see Howie in the gloom of the pines' shadows, just the frequent reflection of the sword as it turned over and over.

"Cocalor dand, dand ha ran."

He turned the corner, brushing Hillary as he slid by the hole. The goat was spinning ever so slowly. He stopped it and positioned himself behind the carcass and the branches at its feet. He took one look at Hillary. Her eyes had the bright glaze of something that was being tortured to death.

The silhouette of the corner of the wall steadily grew as Howie came around it. He inched his way forward, holding the blade in front. His foot distinguished the edge of the shelf from air, and he turned the corner.

"Hokkani hukkani dook."

Howie almost lost his balance as he heard the voice and saw the shadowy figure directly in front of him. He exhaled faintly and moved forward again, watching the white shirt. As he stepped past Hillary hidden in her niche, the sword appeared as a coil of light high above his head.

"Don't!" Hillary broke out.

Howie halted and turned. They touched and looked directly at each other's face. Hillary screamed.

Roman saw Howie changing the angle of his cut so she wouldn't be protected by the wall. There was no way he could reach them over the hole. He pushed the goat. It swung too lazily to Howie, and he saw it coming. He had plenty of time to set himself and swing at its belly. The blade sliced through the intestines like butter. There was no backbone left; it had already been chopped through. The lower half of the carcass dropped through the branches into the hole. Howie staggered forward, propelled by the momentum of his swing. His front foot slipped over the edge of the hole and he grabbed the swinging torso. He managed to pull himself nearly out when the strain finally snapped the damaged rope. He and the top of the goat vanished together down the hole. His last act was to throw the sword aside so that he wouldn't land on it.

They sat and waited on the ledge for two hours. In all that time there wasn't a sound from the hole. At last the dark began washing out of the sky, not so much as if day were entering victoriously as if night simply let go. The lower woods were still in shadow when the tops of the pines veered toward the dawn. Roman let himself down in the hole. It was obvious Howie could outwait them all.

He was on the bottom, his arms locked around the goat. The sword lay harmlessly beside them along with the pandy legs it had cut off. Howie didn't move as Roman passed the sword up to Hillary or didn't start as Roman turned him over. His last surprise was in his face. Roman quickly shielded him and rearranged it, closing the eyes and drawing the corners of the mouth down. It was more than he could do for the girl on the aluminum table, but Howie still looked like a broken bust put back, subtly, completely ruined. Roman pulled the goat out of his arms. Its absence left two spongy holes in Howie's chest where its horns had cradled. The animal's gold, gun-slit eyes caught the first light of day as it broke over the pines.

"Howie sacrificed himself," Hillary said.

24

"Now that makes sense," Isadore decided, "He wanted to get the girl's money; that's why he framed her old man. Don't give me any of this hocus-pocus stuff."

Roman and Isadore were making slow progress down Centre Street to department headquarters. Every time Isadore wanted to make a point he stopped and jabbed a stubby index finger into Roman's arm. Pedestrians took second looks at the round policeman and the dark man with the patch on his head.

Roman snapped his fingers.

"I never thought of that."

Isadore scowled. "Sure. Well, you better think of this: Your testimony's the only thing between those kids and a healthy sentence. They're only out of trouble as long as you are, at least until the trial is over. So stay clean." His finger beat a tarantella on Roman's shoulder.

Roman countered by whistling a mazurka. It gave him a headache, but it kept Isadore from asking any more questions. They went into headquarters and got on an elevator.

"Lousy home life," Isadore relented. "That's what did it.

They wouldn't have swallowed any of that stuff if they had good homes."

The psychological explanation seemed to be a respectable compromise between Roman's demon theory and the usual economic motivation. "Don't give me any more tales about the devil. It's not the sort of case breakdown that the captain likes."

"You're right."

"I can't say that a werewolf in the shape of this Howie tried to start a new wave of human sacrifices. It looks a little funny on the file cards. You'll have to bear with us if we say Howard Washington Hale, thirty-two, mental discharge from the Marine Corps, schizoid, superior intelligence, tried to work a new racket. Okay?"

"You're the detective," Roman said as he ushered Isadore into his own office.

"I keep reminding myself."

They sat down, and Isadore pushed over a sheaf of papers for Roman to sign. Roman went over the statements word by word. Isadore glanced covertly at the men at the other desks. He took off his jacket, cleaned his fingernails and picked his teeth, but Roman didn't hurry. Isadore even took his hat off. A few of the other officers were sitting up and smirking by now.

"Will you sign one of these goddamn things?" Isadore whispered. "You're making a fool out of me. You're on our side, remember?"

Roman didn't fool about papers. He took his cigarettes and pushed them across the desk to Isadore. Isadore refused and shoved a stick of gum in his mouth. The damn Gypsy had the funniest quirks, he thought.

Isadore meditated upon society in general, on fathers and sons, Gypsies and non-Gypsies. The curious thing, he decided, was that the person who had come out best was Grey's fellow antique dealer, Sloan. Charges dropped, daughter safe, troublesome girlfriend out of the way, insurance money paid.

"This one isn't for me," Roman said.

He handed one of the papers to Isadore. It was a bulletin from Boston, and Isadore wondered if some supernatural signal had prompted the thought about Sloan. The dealer was poisoned, a suicide in his workshop an hour after he was released. According to the first report, the dealer's mouth and throat were covered with gold paint. Roman had written in the margin the word "orpiment."

"What does that mean?" Isadore asked.

"It means he became an antique. You see, some people do believe in magic."

He started signing the papers. Isadore picked up the bulletin and got up to go to the teletype room, hoping that nothing else strange and illogical had happened. He crossed his fingers.

MURDER...
MAYHEM...
MYSTERY...

From Ballantine

MYSTERY and SUSPENSE

RUTH RENDELL

AL-40